I0546147

MR. BIG DEAL

THE MR. BIG SHOT SERIES: BOOK FOUR

S. E. LUND

MR. BIG DEAL

The Mr. Big Shot Series: Book Four

Disclaimer: The material in this book is for mature audiences only and contains graphic content. It is intended only for those aged 18 and older.

Sign up for the S. E. Lund Mailing List and get free eBooks, updates on new releases, upcoming sales and giveaways as well as sneak previews before everyone else. She hates spam and will never share your information!

Sign up below:

http://eepurl.com/1Wcz5

Created with Vellum

CHAPTER 1

Alexa

∽

"ONE NIGHT ISN'T ENOUGH."

My mother's voice was disapproving. She stood in front of her laptop on a FaceTime call with me, her hands on her hips.

"You two need two nights away, minimum, so make sure you pump enough milk for as many feedings as you'll miss."

I hesitated. Could I really leave Leif for two whole days? He was only six weeks old...

"I don't know if I can do that," I said, sitting in front of my own laptop. My mom had sent me a message that she wanted to FaceTime and offered to give Luke and I a weekend off so we could have some time to ourselves. Leif was now six weeks old and was doing well by all standards.

Luke and I were tired, but happy. We'd barely had a day

to ourselves since Leif was born, but both of us were glad to have the chance to stay home with him during his first year. We knew that many families didn't have that luxury.

"You can feed him all day Friday, and your dad and I will give him his evening feed and the one in the middle of the night. If you pump enough bottles, you can spend the day together, Saturday night, and then come back Sunday. We'll be fine."

"I'll have to pump all week so that we have enough bottles. That's…" I counted the number of feeds between Friday evening and Sunday evening. "That's at least sixteen bottles…"

"If you'd supplement with formula, you wouldn't have to pump so much."

"We're not ready for that yet. Maybe when Leif is six months old, we'll introduce him to some formula. Not until."

"Okay," Mom said with a sigh. "Have it your way. If you wait until Saturday, you'll be so tired, you won't be able to enjoy your first evening and night alone. You know what I mean. You'll both sleep like logs. You want to have a nice romantic dinner and then spend the evening together enjoying each other's company."

I knew what she meant, of course. Luke and I could spend the evening enjoying each other's bodies, which we had rarely done since Leif came into our lives. The first six weeks I spent healing and trying to adjust to twice a night feedings.

"We'll be happy just to sleep through the night if possible."

She clicked her tongue in disapproval. "You'll have to get up and pump, so I bet you won't sleep through the night."

"I tell you what," I said. "We'll go on Friday, and I can nip home once during the day on Saturday to feed Leif. That way, you won't have to do so many feeds. I can do the same on Sunday, and then we can go for a sail in the afternoon. That would be really nice."

"Deal," Mom said, and I could hear the relief in her voice. "You can feed Leif, go out for a nice meal in a real restaurant, then go to the hotel, have a good unbroken sleep, and then come by in the afternoon to feed Leif. Rinse, repeat. Your dad and I are happy to stay with Leif both nights."

"Okay," I said and took in a deep breath. "How about next Friday? That will give me time to bank some bottles of milk, so you'll have enough. Two a day should do the trick."

"I'll leave that part to you," Mom said with a chuckle. "In my day, we didn't worry about pumping because we started to bottle feed as soon as possible."

"I know. Thanks for the offer. I'm sure Luke will be happy."

We said goodbye and I ended the call, smiling as I thought about the chance to spend a weekend alone with Luke, and most of all, to get a really great sleep.

That had been the one thing — besides sex — missing in our lives.

Frankly, at that point in the new motherhood thing, sleep was what I missed the most because Luke was always there right beside me. Sex was the very last thing I thought about. I was sure that Luke was still in need, because other than sleep interruption, he wasn't as physically affected as I was, but he was discreet enough that I didn't hear him taking matters into his own hands, so to speak.

For the next week, I pumped as many bottles of breast

milk as I could, placing them in the freezer so they'd stay fresh for our weekend away.

When Friday came, Luke and I were nervous about leaving Leif, but excited about the chance to eat a meal in a restaurant and actually sleep. We planned on going to bed at ten o'clock, and sleeping until at least three in the morning, when I figured I'd have to wake and pump. Then, another six or seven hours of sleep after that.

We'd both feel right as rain.

Mom and Dad showed up at six on the dot and were happy to take Leif from my reluctant arms.

"You kids go now," my father said, shooing us out the front door. "Take your overnight bags and git. Your mom and I know what we're doing. You'll be fine. See you tomorrow!"

He literally pushed us through the front entrance, smiling as he did.

"Thanks, Dad," I said and gave him a quick kiss. I glanced back at my mother, who was holding Leif and staring lovingly at his little mostly bald head.

I knew she would be very happy to have him all to herself all weekend. My dad would be lucky to get any Leif time and I smiled as I imagined them fighting over who got to hold and change and bathe and feed him.

We had a lovely meal at a local seafood restaurant, then checked in at the at the East Hampton Bed and Breakfast that we had booked along the coast father north, in a room overlooking Gardiners Bay. We literally fell into bed at nine-thirty, and without much fanfare, kissed each other and fell asleep.

I woke up in the middle of the night in a room of total darkness with the exception of the light from the clock radio on the bedside table, which read three thirty, and a thin sliver of moonlight from under the heavy curtain at the window.

At first, I didn't know where the heck I was…

All I knew was that my breasts felt like twin watermelons and both nipples were leaking.

It was feeding time.

Then, I remembered…

I was in the bed and breakfast. Leif was back at the beach house with my mother and father.

"You okay?" Luke sat up beside me, his voice hushed. He was as exhausted as me. He switched on the lamp beside the bed. "Time to pump?"

"Yes," I said and sat on the side of the bed, acutely aware of the wet spots on my lacy nighty. "I guess Mom and Dad will be up now feeding Leif."

I glanced down and touched my nightgown. The nursing bra and nursing pads hadn't managed to protect it.

Oh, well. At least I had ample milk, which was a godsend.

Luke went to the bathroom and switched on the light. While I got out the sterilized bottles from the bottle bag, and removed the pump from its case, Luke had a quick pee and then I heard water running while he washed his hands.

He came back into the room, fully naked, his delightfully buff physique not yet taken on the Man Bod appearance that John warned it would.

He pulled on some boxer briefs and came over to help me.

I was lucky to have such a supportive spouse and I knew it. Maybe all men of our generation were as interested in taking part in the daily life of parenthood. I knew that my father missed out a lot when he was so busy with his career while I was growing up. He intended to make up for it by being as involved in Leif's life as he could be.

I plugged the breast pump into the socket on the night-stand and then proceeded to pump my breasts, emptying them of the milk that would go immediately into the small refrigerator in the dining room area of the suite. Luke sat beside me and put an arm around my shoulder. "Six hours straight. I think that's a record."

"I know," I said and smiled. "I feel positively half-refreshed."

He leaned over and kissed me. "We get to sleep in today. I feel like a king. Your mother and father are angels of mercy."

I laughed. "Don't kid yourself. They love it. My father never had the chance to be with me much while I was a baby, so he's eating the granddad thing up."

"It's actually really sweet," Luke said and sighed. "I wish my stepmother wasn't such a bitch and didn't have a grudge against you. That way, we could all be one big happy family, the way I always imagined."

I exhaled heavily. I wanted us all to make amends and be happy, but Luke just didn't think he could forgive her for what she'd done to hurt me — to hurt us. He insisted that releasing the video of Blaine assaulting me was a bridge too far. We'd talked about it, wondering what we would do if she did come around and apologized for everything, and was on good behavior going forward.

"I can't take her back," Luke had said. "Not now. Not after what she did."

So, my parents and Luke's Stepdad Grant would have to do. Luckily, Grant was on good terms with us, so at least he would be invited to family get-togethers and holidays. I wanted Leif to know what it was like to have a big family around him, supporting him throughout his life.

I filled up two bottles worth and when finished, I handed them to Luke, who dutifully put them in the refrigerator. I put the pump away, got up and had a pee, and then went back to bed. Luke was back under the covers and when I snuck in beside him after replacing the nipple pads with fresh ones, he pulled me into his arms for a kiss.

"Feeling better? Less like squeezing two basketballs between your arms?"

"Yes, thanks," I said and snuggled into his embrace. "I love being able to nurse Leif, but honestly, I'm looking forward to when he feeds less, and you can get up and give him a bottle while I sleep."

"You know I'd be happy to do it now," Luke said defensively. "I told you I would…"

"No," I said quickly, sensing the hurt in Luke's voice. "I want to keep nursing at night until he's older and my milk supply is more certain."

"Okay, if you're sure. Kaylee said that you could let me do one feed in the night as long as you pumped."

Kaylee was our new Nurse Practitioner, who helped get me settled back home with Leif after the hospital visit.

"I know, but I want to wait until Leif is older. Kaylee said that at six months, babies often stop feeding as often at night, so we could try at that point. Until then, I'll be fine."

Luke kissed me forehead. "Okay, but the offer stands if you change your mind."

With that, we snuggled down and soon fell back to sleep.

CHAPTER 2

Alexa

WHEN I NEXT WOKE UP, MY BREASTS WERE ONCE AGAIN full and aching. I glanced at the clock radio and saw that it was nearly seven thirty in the morning.

Time to get up.

I slipped out of bed, checking on Luke as I did. He was lying on his stomach, a pillow over his head as usual. I took the breast pump and two bottles into the bathroom, intending to pump without waking up Luke if I could help it.

I went to the second bathroom nearer to the kitchen area and closed the door before switching on the light. In the brightness of the overhead lights, I looked as tired as I still felt. There were bags under my eyes and my hair looked like an old broomstick made of straw, with bits and pieces sticking out from my loose braid.

I really did need a holiday.

Luke and I were really lucky — luckier than most new parents. We didn't have to worry about money or jobs, with Luke doing most of his work via Zoom or Skype. I was on a leave of absence from Columbia and didn't have to worry about studying or writing papers. We had a beautiful house in Westhampton Beach and a housekeeper who kept the place spotless and did our grocery shopping.

All we had to worry about was Leif and sleep.

Leif was doing great, hitting all his developmental targets, and was starting to show a bit of a personality. He smiled a lot and I loved it when he got all coy, like his whole body smiled back at me.

I loved him so much...

I was able to pump both my breasts without waking Luke. Then, I went to the master suite bathroom and turned on the shower and stepped inside, glad of the hot spray, which helped to wake me up. I was able to finish my shower and get dried off and dressed without waking up Luke, which was my goal. Once I was finished, I went to the kitchen area and brewed a pot of fresh coffee.

The scent of coffee was what finally woke Luke. I heard him rustling around in the bedroom, having a shower and then getting dressed. On my part, I stood at the patio door leading to the veranda and watched the clouds on the horizon. It was a hot hazy summer made a bit cooler by our closeness to the ocean. I would be glad for September and October and the relief from the heat and humidity.

Luke was still inside the shower, humming to himself.

I stripped off my clothes and joined him, my arms around his neck. We kissed and stood in the shower for a while, just enjoying our wet skin pressed against each other.

"This is nice," he said. "I miss this."

"Me, too."

We washed each other, and then, he turned the shower off, pulling me out of the stall and onto the bathmat.

"You're so sexy, so ripe and full, I want you right now."

"I want you, too," I said, and he took my hand, pulling me into the bedroom. Before I could protest, he kissed me, his arms slipping around me, pulling me against him. I wrapped my legs around him, to encourage him and that did it. He pushed me onto the bed, lying on top of me.

"You are so beautiful," he said, taking my hands in his.

I looked up into his eyes – his very determined eyes — and saw his lust and his love. His hair fell into his eyes in that sexy way, and he was breathing fast. I knew he wanted me.

I was so ready for him, my flesh swollen and wet. I couldn't wait for his hardness to fill me up completely.

"You sure you're ready?" he whispered. "We can do other things if not."

I shook my head. "I'm more than ready. It's been more than six weeks."

He kissed my neck. "You can say no, and I'll stop. I don't want to hurt you."

"I want this," I said. "I want you. I need *you*."

He I kissed me again, deeply this time, claiming my mouth, sucking my tongue into his mouth while he ground his erection against my sex. My back arched at the sensations, and soon, I was panting, needing to feel him enter me.

He pulled off my nightgown, so that I lay naked beneath him. He ran his hands over my body, from my hips to my waist, and then cupped one breast in a hand.

"You are so lush," he whispered, then kissed his way down from my jaw to my neck. I glanced down and was afraid that I'd leak because of arousal, but so far, nothing and I tried to relax.

I closed my eyes as he ran his tongue all around the curve of my breasts then swiped it over the hard bud of one nipple. I groaned and arched my back, pressing my breasts, unable to stop myself.

"Please," I whispered, my eyes closed, my body throbbing with need. "I need you now."

When I looked in his eyes, he was smiling, enjoying my pleading.

"Be patient," he said, his voice amused. "I like it when you beg for it."

I smiled. "Don't get too used to it."

He ran his tongue down my belly to my navel, and then lower to my thighs, which were spread. He pressed them open even wider and ran his tongue all around my clit without touching it, driving me wild with need. Finally, when I thought I would cry out from desire, he stroked it fully, pressing his tongue flat against it.

I couldn't help but move my hips, needing the sensation.

"So wet," he whispered, pressing my legs farther apart. "Nice and wet."

He licked me slowly, running his tongue over me until I was shuddering.

"Oh, God," I groaned, my orgasm so close. He quickly entered me and the sensation of his erection sliding into me sent me over the top, my body spasming around him.

He began to slow thrust inside me while I panted, my orgasm waning.

"You okay?" he asked, his voice breathless.

"Yes," I said, my eyes closed. "I'm wonderful."

Then, he thrust with more urgency, and soon, he was gritting his teeth, his face red with desire. I could feel his cock so hard as he came, his body straining above me, then he ejaculated, his body spasming.

Finally, he collapsed on top of me, exhaling in pure pleasure.

I slipped my arms around his neck and pulled him close as he panted.

When he rose up and looked in my eyes, I smiled.

"Looks like sex is back on the menu, boys."

He grinned and kissed me, enjoying my Lord of the Rings reference, as I knew he would.

I was afraid of pain during our first lovemaking session, but Luke knew what he was doing.

I closed my eyes and relaxed, glad that I was finally back.

I smiled and lay there while he got up and went to the closet. I grabbed my robe and pulled it on, and then removed the wet bedspread, hanging it over the shower curtain rod to dry off.

WHILE LUKE DRESSED, I went to the kitchen and poured us each a cup of coffee. While he got ready, I thought about the future. Labor Day was coming up and we would have a weekend party at the beach house, inviting all family and friends to attend and enjoy a barbecue. Since Eric had been arrested and was facing the loss of his driver's license and other penalties, we didn't expect to see or hear much from him. While we still had security in place to watch the property and go with us whenever we went away from home, I felt a lot safer knowing that the police had finally dealt with Luke's former brother-in-law.

The only remaining stains on our beautiful life were Mrs. Marshall and Blaine.

Neither were far from my thoughts.

Blaine had been arrested and charged with attempted murder, but his bail had been set at $500,000 and he had made bail, thanks to a wealthy family member who came forward and paid the bond.

He was supposedly waiting for his court date, which was in the distant future, but until he was found guilty and put in jail, we felt that we were at risk from him.

He'd tried to kill Candace.

There was no reason to think he wouldn't try to kill me or Luke.

Why he got bail, I would never know, but apparently, innocent until guilty meant that in New York State, you got bail even for a violent offence.

Thankfully, Seneca Investments had stuck by Luke and were now a partner in the space business, bringing with them a lot of investment dollars. I held out hope that Luke and Adam Pierce would be able to find other angel investors who would make the venture a success. While I knew nothing about the space industry, Luke knew everything and was going to make his mark in life as a space entrepreneur, not yet competing with Elon for public recognition, but at least earning the respect of those in the industry.

"Hey, Mrs. Marshall," Luke said, coming up behind me and slipping his arms around me. He kissed my neck. "Are you feeling as good as me? I needed that."

"I needed it, too," I said and turned around in his arms. "That other four hours of sleep really refreshed me, and I'm no longer tired."

"Good. I feel like taking the boat out today before we go

back home. What do you say?" He kissed me and then stroked my cheek. "Feel like a quick trip around the island? We don't have to be back home until after supper, based on the bottles of breast milk you left for your mom and dad."

I smiled and handed Luke a cup of coffee. "Your wish is my command."

"Oh, really?" Luke wagged his eyebrows meaningfully. I knew what that meant. Luke felt a burning desire.

For the sea.

"Yes, really. Let's eat and get to the slip in Patchogue. We haven't taken Phoenix out for a long time."

"I know," Luke said. "Security doesn't like the idea of us going out without some kind of backup. I told Frank that it was highly unlikely that Blaine or Eric will chase us around the Island in a speedboat. I think we can do it safely now. We've heard and seen nothing out of order. Hopefully, Blaine has given up his dreams of vengeance."

I shrugged, not quite as optimistic as Luke.

Blaine had very little left in his life now that he was waiting for his trial. My father said that made Blaine more dangerous, not less. Our only hope was that Blaine found someone else to dominate and would leave me and Luke and Leif alone. Blaine was still a threat and was the primary reason Luke kept the security firm on the payroll. I had almost become used to having so much security around me, but there were moments when it still shocked me. I hoped Blaine had just given up, deciding that there were better victims to find and abuse. He'd already done enough damage - to Candace and to my nerves and reputation.

"We have to live our lives," Luke said. "I'm keeping security in place, but I think we can safely take the Phoenix out for a run without worrying too much. If Frank insists, he can rent a boat from the local yacht club and follow us around the island."

I nodded. "Let's get breakfast and then go. I can't wait to get out on the water."

"Me, too," Luke said, smiling. I saw the fatigue evaporate in his eyes at the thought of sailing and knew it was the right decision.

With that, we grabbed our things and left the room for the restaurant and breakfast.

We had the whole day ahead of us, and I intended to enjoy every minute of my time with Luke.

CHAPTER 3

Luke

Being on the water was just what Alexa and I needed to feel refreshed and ready for the week ahead. I was determined to go once a month at least — more if possible and if Mom and Dad Dixon were able to look after Leif while we were on the water.

One day soon, Leif would be old enough to come with us, and I so looked forward to that day when I could teach my son all about sailing.

There wasn't enough wind to do much sailing, so we used the twin motors to propel us along the coast, enjoying the ocean breeze such as it was and the salty smell of the surf. I stood at the helm and steered the boat while Alexa lounged on the deck in front of my window. It was a lovely view. Alexa's body was still lush from her pregnancy, and she'd been sunning herself on and off during the summer while Leif slept so that her usually pale skin was now a

S. E. LUND

beautiful golden brown. She may have felt exhausted from
the previous six weeks of new motherhood, but to me, she
was just as beautiful as ever — if not more so. There was
even a cute spray of freckles across the bridge of her nose
that I completely adored.

Motherhood suited her.

I felt so lucky that I had accidentally sent her that email,
including one too-many x's in the email address. If I had
been more careful, I would never have met her and would
probably still be a bachelor looking for Ms. Right in all the
wrong places.

There was no one else exactly like her. I was damn
lucky, and I knew it. I would do anything and everything to
keep her happy and by my side.

AFTER ABOUT AN HOUR OF TRAVEL, we found a deserted
cove along the coast, and I anchored Phoenix and went out
to where Alexa lay sunning herself.

"Feel like a swim? It's getting really warm."

"Sounds great," Alexa replied and stood up. I took her
all in, noting the slight swell of her belly, the ample breasts,
and rounded hips and could have taken her inside to the
bedroom to ravish her. Instead, I took her hand, and we
went to the side of the Phoenix where the water was deeper
and both of us jumped in, still holding hands.

The water was a shock. Even in August, it was cold and
made even more so because of the heat of the air.

Alexa came up for air beside me and sputtered. "Oh,
my God it's so freaking cold!"

"It is," I replied and swam beside her, treading water.
"It's invigorating."

"Invigorating? It's freezing! I might go into shock if I stay in much longer."

She was smiling, so I knew she was just exaggerating for comic effect. We swam around for a few moments and then floated beside each other, staring up at the clear blue sky.

"I wish we were in Bora Bora," Alexa said with a sigh. "Those were some of my happiest moments in my entire life."

"Me, too. We'll take Leif there as soon as he's old enough to enjoy it. Now that we can do everything online, I can travel without worrying."

"When I'm finished my classes," Alexa added. "I can do my research and writing online, too."

"It's settled," I said and swam over to her, my arms around her. We treaded water together and then kissed. "When Leif is able to sit up on his own, we'll take a trip. Maybe not in Phoenix. We can fly to Bora Bora and rent a sailboat at the local marina if we want. Stay in our favorite port for a month. Or longer," I added, thinking it would be nice to spend a few months in the South Pacific.

"We're so lucky," Alexa said with a sigh. "To have the freedom to travel. It's a dream come true."

"You have to finish your PhD first, so we can travel around the world and visit all the European capitals like you wanted. Prague. Bern. Amsterdam. London. Paris."

"Istanbul," Alexa added. "I want to sit in a cafe in Istanbul and drink Turkish coffee and eat authentic Turkish food."

"Yes, then on to Athens, the Greek Islands, and Rome. I want to see Rome. Carthage. Algiers. I want to see it all. Can you imagine taking a train across Europe?"

"The Orient Express. Oh, and the Trans-Siberian Railway," she added.

"We could start a travel vlog and I could become a travel influencer instead of boring old space entrepreneur."

She grinned. "Not on your life." She kissed me. "You're a space entrepreneur. You can just be a world traveler on top of it."

"Sounds perfect."

We kissed again and I felt my body respond to her breasts pressed against me.

She felt my body respond as well and narrowed her eyes. "Feel like a nap after our swim?"

I grinned. "I thought you'd never ask."

She led the way back to Phoenix and climbed up the ladder, her delicious body on full display while I followed her.

I couldn't wait to feel her naked and aroused next to me on the bed. I knew once we got back to the beach house, and back into our daily routine with Leif, we wouldn't feel quite as relaxed and free as we did at that moment, and I didn't want to waste it.

Luckily, she felt the same and so we stripped off each other's bathing suits and then spent the next hour teasing and delighting each other.

~

WHEN WE WERE BOTH FINISHED, lying on our backs staring up through the skylight above the bed, I smiled.

"That was very good, Mrs. Marshall. Very good."

"It was, Mr. Marshall. I think my need has been growing for the past week, despite the fatigue and loss of sleep."

"So, I know the way into your panties now, do I? A good sleep is all it takes?"

She rolled over and laid her head on my shoulder. I could see her smile. "That and all your sweet talk about traveling the world."

We moored the boat and drove back home to Westhampton, where Alexa took some time to feed Leif and I sat with Mr. Dixon on the patio and talked about the space business.

When Alexa was finished, she brought Leif out for me to change and I was happy to take him to the table where I laid out a change pad and did my duty, changing his diaper and putting him in a clean onesie.

"All done," I said and went out to the patio where everyone was sitting. We spent the next half hour talking to them and sharing time with Leif.

Then, we said goodbye and left once more, driving along the coast, taking in the sights and enjoying the rest of our day together. We went to a local seafood restaurant for our dinner, enjoying fresh shrimp and crab.

We spent the evening at the B&B, watching some sports, then after a bubble bath and a nice slow session of lovemaking, we went to sleep around midnight.

As with the previous night, Alexa woke up and had to pump once in the night, but we quickly fell back to sleep.

We woke the next morning, and then repeated our previous day's activities, with a nice brunch at the local restaurant, then a sail along the coast.

When that was done, we packed up our bags and drove back to the beach house, our forty hours of vacation over.

When we arrived back, Alexa's dad was waiting with baby Leif in his arms. He smiled when he saw us.

"Back so soon?" he said, his wide smile telling me that he had been enjoying himself with his grandson. "We could have done another twenty-four hours you know.

There are a couple extra bottles, and if you fed him now..."

"No, we're relaxed and refreshed and ready to be parents again," Alexa said, giving him a smile. She took Leif in her arms gently because he was sleeping and when he was back in his mother's embrace, he woke and started snuffling like he could smell her.

"I guess he knows who his mother is," Mr. Dixon said with a grin. "The bottle is good enough, but as they say, breast is best."

"That it is," Alexa said. When Leif let out a loud cry, she turned to me and smiled. "And like Pavlov's Dog, when I hear him cry, my milk lets down."

"Nature is wonderful," I replied and carried our overnight bags inside the house.

It was good to be back to the beach house and our regular routine, as much as I enjoyed our nights away. I loved my life with Alexa and Leif and wouldn't exchange it for anything.

While Alexa fed Leif, Mr. and Mrs. Dixon and I sat in the great room while they both finished a cup of coffee.

"Frankly, we needed the caffeine to stay awake," Mrs. Dixon said with a laugh. She looked a bit tired, her blue eyes a bit bleary. "But we loved being with Leif and we're glad he's such a happy camper. Alexa was a colicky baby at this age, so we were pretty sleepless and stressed until she seemed to get over it at four months and started sleeping through the night."

"She slept through the night at four months?" I asked, incredulously.

"Yes," Mrs. Dixon said and smiled guiltily. "That's when I stopped nursing and switched to formula. I know that you young people don't approve, but we finally got a good night's sleep and Alexa's colic seemed to pass. Maybe my milk wasn't rich enough? I don't know but it was pretty smooth sailing from then on."

I nodded. "We figure we'll get there at about six months if we're lucky. Thankfully, Leif is pretty happy most of the time. Not fussy."

"He must have inherited your temperament," Mr. Dixon said with a chuckle. "Alexa was a fussy little thing, always squirming and wanting more to drink."

I turned and watched her feeding Leif, his face pressed against her breast, his hand on it like an embrace. She was staring down at him with such love in her eyes, that I felt my heart swell with my own love for them both.

When she was finished feeding Leif, she handed him to me for the burp. I quickly placed a cloth diaper over my shoulder and proceeded to pat him on the back until he let out a huge burp. Luckily, nothing else came up so I didn't have to clean up and then I sat him up and let him stare around at his grandpa and grandma while Alexa went to make us some decaf coffee.

WE FOLLOWED them both to the front door when it was time for them to head back to the city.

"Thanks again for doing this," I said.

"Yes, thanks so much," Alexa added. "We got a nice break and spent some time on the water."

"The time alone together is so important," Mrs. Dixon said and leaned over to kiss Leif on the head. She then gave me a quick kiss and one-armed hug. Mr. Dixon did the same with me and then Alexa hugged them both.

We watched them walk to their car and then waved as they drove off.

"Well, Mrs. Marshall. That was a very nice escape."

"It was," Alexa said and closed the door. "Back to the real world, which I love more than anything."

"Me, too."

LEIF SEEMED ESPECIALLY fussy that night, perhaps because he'd missed Alexa and the breast over the past twenty-four hours, and she was up twice in the night with him.

"Let me get up and at least give him a bottle," I said when Leif woke up the second time.

"No, no," Alexa said. "I want to hold him and feed him. I think it will reassure him that all is well and he's safe."

"Okay, but the offer stands."

I watched as she slipped out of bed and went to his room to feed him. In a moment, I could hear on the baby monitor the sound of him snuffling as he searched for the breast, found it and began nursing. I got up and had a pee, then went to the door to the nursery. Alexa hummed a soft lullaby while she rocked in the rocker beside his crib.

It was a picture-perfect sight. We had a nightlight made up of the constellations that slowly turned around, making the ceiling look like a night sky. Alexa was sitting in the rocking chair in her nightie, one shoulder strap pulled down, Leif's little face pressed against her breast.

My two people — my favorite two people in the world. I couldn't wait for Leif to grow up and I could teach him everything I knew about life, and I could learn from him how to be a good loving father.

I didn't think I could possibly feel any more love and happiness than at that moment in time and wanted to capture it, so I went to get my camera, adjusted the settings for low light, and then snapped a photo of the two of them, the stars above their head.

One day, I would show it to him, but until then, it would be the screensaver to my cell and on my laptop, to remind me of just how lucky and happy I was.

CHAPTER 4

August 2019

Alexa

≈

Life went back to normal over the next couple of months.

I worked on my dissertation research, Luke did a lot of FaceTime calls with John, and the girls came out a couple of times for a visit on the weekends, enjoying the beach house with us during the last days of Summer.

Mom and Dad had decided to give us a night off once a month, and Luke and I agreed that it was more than just a treat — it was a necessity. Our next night off was coming up on the weekend, and I was excited, planning our stay at a hotel close to where Phoenix was so that we could take her out for a long sail. Hopefully, the wind would be in our favour, and we would be able to get some great sailing.

We kept our security detail in place just to be safe

despite there being no word about Blaine. Occasionally, I'd catch sight of a strange vehicle in the driveway and remember why it was there when I saw the small logo on the side door. The logo was unobtrusive, and only we would know it was from the security company. There was nothing besides a stylized eagle with his wings spread to identify the company. It made me feel safer, if not sad that my life had come to a point where I needed a security service to protect me, Luke and Leif from Blaine.

Still, I was lucky that we could afford it. Some women faced abusive exes all on their own, with only a restraining order in place. Knowing Blaine as we did now, that would never be enough to keep him away from us. Only a show of muscle worked.

I hope it stayed that way.

The girls were coming out on Friday night for an overnight stay, so they could spend time with me and Leif while Luke stayed in town overnight for a late meeting with some potential investors. He had to wine and dine them, and so decided to stay in the city. He suggested that I invite Candace and my other two besties out to keep me company. Mara could make it, but Jan couldn't. It would still be fun and the three of us would have a barbecue, spend the day on the small beach in front of the beach house, and then stay up and watch the latest episode of whatever was hot on the streaming services.

I was looking forward to a night with the girls, and wished Jan could be with us, but she had a hot date. Brandon Wright was his name, but we liked to joke she finally met Mr. Right and she loved it. He traveled a lot for his job in international finance, so when he was in town, she said she was his and only his. I couldn't expect her to break a hot date with Mr. Right. Luke was having a shower, getting ready to leave and Leif was taking his afternoon nap.

Luke came out of the bedroom closet, wearing one of his best suits. It was dark grey, and he wore a black silk tie. The ensemble set off his bright blue eyes and made him look like the hottest space cadet of all time.

"How do I look?" he asked and adjusted his lapels. "Good enough to merit several millions of dollars in investment?"

"You look marvellous, darling," I quipped. "More like a billion dollars."

"Good," he said and ran his fingers through his a-bit-too-long hair, which he had neglected to get cut over the past few months. The bangs hung into his eyes, and he had to continually sweep them back in a very sexy way — sexy, at least, to me. "Remind me when we get back from our date night to get a haircut."

"I don't know," I said and went to him, slipping my arms around him from behind as he stood primping in front of the mirror. "I think I prefer you with those bangs. They make you look so Emo."

"Emo?" He glanced at himself, turning his head from side to side. "That won't do. Should I get a pair of scissors and cut them myself? I don't want Mr. Adam Pierce of Seneca Investments to think I'm some Emo dude..."

I laughed and squeezed him. "Use some gel. That'll keep your hair in place. You'll look like the Wolf of Wall Street instead of a Space Entrepreneur, but better that than an Emo dude."

"Good idea," Luke said and turned around in my arms, bending down to kiss me, his hands cupping my face. "Thanks for not minding me staying overnight. I know

Adam wants to enjoy the Manhattan night life scene while he's here from Seattle."

"No problem," I replied and kissed him back. "I get my bestie time, so I'm happy."

We hugged closely for a moment, and it was then I heard snuffling noises on the baby monitor. Leif was waking up.

"Duty calls," I said and leaned up on my toes to kiss Luke once more.

He let me go and followed me into the nursery. The light was low, the curtains and blinds closed and the night light on, illuminating the room in stars and galaxies.

"Hey, there," I said and picked Leif up. He stretched and wriggled in my arms, and then smiled when I brought him out into the hallway, and he saw Luke.

"There's my boy," Luke said and leaned over to kiss Leif on the forehead. "I'll miss you."

"You better go," I said and held up my Apple watch to show Luke the time. "Your ride will be waiting."

"Yes, I better."

I followed Luke out into the entryway and watched him slip on his shoes and then grab his briefcase and overnight bag.

"Goodbye, my two favorite people in all the world," Luke said and kissed us both once more. "I'll call you later when I get into bed if you want."

"Sure," I said. "I'll probably go to sleep around midnight. Call me if you're in by then."

"I'm sure I will be. I'll claim that as a new father, I'm too tired to stay up really late and make sure I'm back in my room by midnight. They'll all understand."

"Okay, but don't leave unless you think it's kosher to. I don't want you to interrupt the evening just because of me.

If you think you should stay out later, go ahead. I won't mind."

"Okay. We'll play it by ear."

He kissed me once more and then left the house. I stood on the front entry with the door open and watched him get into the waiting limo provided by the security service. He waved once and then the limo drove off. The sedan from the security company that would watch over me and the property was still in the driveway, the Eagle crest visible from where I stood.

I felt completely safe.

CHAPTER 5

Luke

THE MEETING WITH THE NEW ANGEL INVESTORS WAS slated to start at six, with a pre-dinner meeting where John and I would do our pitch for Astra Investments and answer any questions the investors had.

Adam Pierce of Seneca Investments was born to wealth and knew how to use it to make more. When he showed an interest in Astra Investments because of our plans to mine the asteroid belt, I knew we were kindred spirits. Like me, Adam wanted to do something with his wealth other than just making more money for its own sake. Money made money doing nothing more than sitting in a basic index fund, but both of us wanted to do something that would last beyond us.

"I know it sounds corny," I said when he asked me for my motivation. "I want to leave something for humanity when I'm gone. When I have the benefit of so much wealth that I did nothing to earn, I feel like I should give part of it back in some way. Mining the asteroid belt sounds like a wacky idea, but it's a literal goldmine of minerals that's free — so far — for the taking, if we can get there and back."

"That's the kicker," Adam said and raised his glass of beer to me. "Getting there and back. That's expensive."

"We have to make it cheaper," I replied. "Get costs down so that it's profitable. Get a rocket system in place, like the rail system used to be. We used the railway to open up the country and get access to the land and resources in the West, so I figure this is more of the same. It's costly to start, but the long-term benefits will far outweigh the initial costs once we get it in place."

"Couldn't agree more," Adam said, and we toasted each other and drank down our beers. "What do you think of the two investors coming here tonight? What's your take on them and their interest?"

Adam shrugged. "My research guy says that Elena Marakova has a lot of her family's rubles that she wants out of Russia and into the USA. She's thinking long-term as well. High up-front cost, steady profits after that. Not a quick fix, in other words."

"Strange to see a woman in the space industry," I said and wondered about her. "She's one of the few."

"She is an astrophysicist, educated in the UK. Her family has money, and she wants to invest in the space race. That's good enough for me."

"Are we sure it's clean money?" I asked, frowning. "I don't want dirty Russian money involved."

Adam raised his eyebrows. "Their fortune came from the shipping industry," he said. "Besides, is there any clean Russian money?"

I laughed ruefully. "Good point. As long as it's legit, that's all I care about in the end."

"It's legit," Adam replied. "I know your views on that."

Our other angel investor hopeful was Jack Tate, who had a fortune to invest and was currently working with a hedge fund. An older man in his late forties, Jack had been in the Air Force, but had joined a hedge fund as an advisor after retiring as a fighter pilot. He wanted to do something with his money and planned to move it into space-based ventures.

"I'm sick of taking over businesses and dismantling them for parts," he said when I asked why he wanted out of the hedge fund. "I want to build, not destroy."

"That's great. I'm looking for visionaries who know that space is the future." I held up my glass of scotch. "That's why I called it Astra. To the stars. Or in Astra's case, the asteroids."

"We were made for each other," Jack said and held up his glass. "Here's to a joint venture between me and Astra. May we make a real difference. On to the asteroids!"

At that moment, Elena Marakova walked in, and she was a stunner as far as women went. Not as beautiful as Alexa, but still, I knew that most men's heads would turn when she walked into the hotel bar where we were holding the get together before the dinner and evening meeting. She looked in her thirties and had dark hair and eyes. A Sophia Loren look-alike, she was very tall and very built, dressed like she was in central casting in the movie the House of Gucci.

"Wow," Jack said, his eyes bugging out. "I saw her photo on the company website, but she was wearing safety glasses, a lab coat and had her hair back. She's quite the beauty."

Jack was single, and I had the sense that he was really

attracted to her. I smiled to myself and watched him for the first hour while we introduced ourselves and talked about the weather, the latest news, and then, of course, the latest sports scores. Surprisingly, Elena kept up with us, citing statistics of her favorite soccer team and hockey team. She drank quite heavily as well, keeping up with Jack drink for drink, but barely showed it.

It looked like a match made in heaven. Elena had a strong Russian accent, but excellent English, and was obviously very intelligent. You don't become an astrophysicist trained in the UK without being a brain.

I thought about Alexa and how she was also a big brain but in a different field. She was also beautiful, but in a completely different way from Elena. Elena had a hard edge to her, which I assumed was from being a woman in a man's world, having to compete with men who were either business types or scientists. Whatever the case, Jack was certainly taken with her.

When we went for dinner, Jack sat beside Elena and kept her busy talking about her family and the business. Adam and I spoke about our own families.

Dinner was enjoyable, and we talked very little of business. Most of the time was spent talking sports, and golf, which I didn't play.

"You don't golf?" Adam asked, smiling. "You really must. It's the way people connect in business. You and I should go out and do nine holes some time. You'll enjoy it. Very relaxing."

"Do you golf?" I asked Jack, who could barely tear his eyes away from Elena.

"Me?" he asked. "Of course, I do. I make sure to lose to whoever I'm golfing with. It has nothing to do with my skill, I'll have you know."

We all laughed at that.

"I never golfed, but I'm willing to try, if that's what ensures I'll get investors," I said and turned to Adam. "Where's a good golf club to join? I'll do it Monday."

Adam proceeded to tell me all about the club he belonged to, and I promised to join and that he and I would have a round of golf in the coming weeks.

"As a new father, I'm sure you'll be glad to get away," Adam said. "All those diapers and bottles. Been there, done that, got the kid almost in college to show for it." He grinned.

Once dinner was over, we moved to a separate room set up like a boardroom, and we ran through plans for Astra-Seneca joint venture. We went over the development of technology that would be critical for the trip to the asteroid belt and mining of the ore. Both Elena and Jack seemed really interested and had good questions and smart comments to make about the future of the industry.

"It's necessary, because we're facing a shortage of rare minerals on earth," Elena said. "Rare minerals we need for computer and new technology to combat global warming."

Jack agreed. I listened to Jack's impassioned talk about lithium batteries and praseodymium and terbium oxide, which were used in magnets and solar batteries, as well as LED and lasers.

These were my people, I realized. They saw the future for what it was — a threat to the advances we had made with technology, and the urgent need to develop space travel so we could continue to grow and develop alternate energies.

The four of us really were super nerds. John would have loved to be there, listening to the discussion about the future of technology. Unfortunately, he was unable to attend due to a last-minute bout of food poisoning.

I was glad that Adam was so willing to sit in on the meeting with me.

We finished the night out and went our separate ways, with Elena and Jack leaving separately, and Adam went to his apartment, and I went to ours. I felt it had been a successful evening, and worth the effort. Investors wanted to know you as a person and not just the numbers on a spreadsheet. In the end, business was a human thing and very social, so it helped if you had people who you felt were kindred spirits to join you in a risky and very costly venture. Money was primary, of course, and if the venture wasn't going to make any, no one would want to invest.

But these were experts who were thinking long-term.

The long term said that Astra-Seneca join venture would be a winner.

I hoped so.

I WENT to the apartment and had a drink of water before going to bed to help dilute the alcohol I'd consumed over the course of the evening — far more than I usually would drink when I was with Alexa or my own friends and family. I fell asleep quickly and when the phone rang in the middle of the night, the first thing I thought of was that something happened to either Leif or Alexa. I jerked awake and grabbed my cell.

It was Gord from the security service.

"Gord, what is it?"

"Sorry to wake you, Sir, but I thought you'd want to know. We had an intruder on the property, but I was able to chase him off before he was able to break in or do any damage. I called police and they are looking for him and will canvass the area in the morning to check on any security cam footage that might help identify him."

"Thanks for calling. How is Mrs. Marshall?"

"She's fine. A bit shaken, as you can understand, but she has her friends with her right now and seems fine."

"Good. I'll be on my way home in five. And Gord? Thanks for looking after my family."

"No thanks required, Sir. This is my job."

"Still, I'm glad we had you there. Who knows what might have happened if they were alone?"

"I'm glad I was here," Gord said and ended the call.

I called Alexa right away, wanting to connect with her, see how she was doing and let her know I was on my way. Of course, she protested that I should stay at the apartment and sleep in, but there was no way I could expect to fall back asleep at that point. I would rather take the limo service home and be with her and Leif than stay in the city.

After I convinced her that it was my choice and I was on my way, and that she should just go to bed and not wait for me to return, I had a quick shower, dressed and then packed up my possessions. I went down to the parking garage where the limo was waiting. I sent a text to our hopeful angel investor, Tom Ellis of Ellis Investments, and his assistant, so they wouldn't be surprised when they realized I'd left the city early and wouldn't be meeting them for breakfast as we planned. We had discussed meeting in the morning, but surely an investor would understand.

As the limo drove off, I sent Adam an email explaining what happened and why I had to leave the city early.

I was sure he'd understand.

CHAPTER 6

Alexa

AFTER LUKE LEFT, I WENT BACK INSIDE AND SAT ON the sofa, preparing to nurse Leif. On the television was some news, so I listened in to talk about whatever was happening in the world outside my little life. I'd been so busy with Leif and my dissertation that I hadn't been following world events much. My mind was busy on the Cold War, and so I hadn't been as attuned to current events as I usually would. One day, when Leif was older and more independent, I would be able to pay more attention to it, but Leif mattered more now than anything else besides Luke.

I had my priorities straight.

Once Leif was finished nursing, I took him back to his room and changed him, then put him in his activity chair while I bustled around in the kitchen getting things ready for the girls, who were due to arrive any moment.

I kept my eye on the security monitor app on my laptop,

which showed an image of the front entry, the driveway and the yard leading to the beach. When I saw a car drive up to the gate, and then proceed into the driveway, I knew that the girls had arrived and went to pick up Leif so we could greet them at the door.

Mara's car drove up to the front entry and out jumped Candace, her curly hair in a high topknot, and some big dangly earrings in her ears. She wore a long sundress and sandals and looked ready for a weekend at the beach. Beside her, Mara reached into the trunk and pulled out two overnight bags.

They turned to the front door, where I stood, and I heard Candace squeal with delight when she saw Leif.

"There he is," she said and came up the steps to me. "Come here, little man. Auntie Candy needs some baby time."

I handed Leif to her, and she hugged and kissed him, her eyes filled with delight. Behind her, Mara came with their overnight bags.

"Hey, Momma," Mara said, smiling, her short dark hair cropped with high bangs, her dark eyes amused at Candace's antics with Leif. "How you doing?"

"I'm great now that you two are here. Come in and get settled in. I'm just getting stuff ready for the barbecue."

For the next fifteen minutes, Candace and Mara took their bags to their rooms, and then came downstairs to help me with preparations for our meal on the patio. The weather was still nice enough that we could sit outside and eat.

While Mara played with Leif, Candace and I did the cooking, placing the steaks and skewers of garlic shrimp on the grill. I'd made a salad beforehand and there was bread, so everything was ready.

"Look what I brought," Candace said, and pulled out a bottle of wine from her bag. "A nice wine to go with the shrimp and steak."

"Looks delicious," I said but shook my head. "Not drinking until I finish nursing Leif and he's on formula. But you two indulge."

"Aww, that's right. You're one of those really responsible moms," Candace said with a pout. "You know my mom drank now and then with me."

"She bottle fed, right?"

"Ahh, yes," Candace said. "Everyone did back then, I guess. Three weeks for the colostrum and that was it. Formula. Mothers these days..."

I smiled and placed the steaks on a plate next to the grilled shrimp. "Dinner is served."

We sat on the patio, taking turns to hold Leif while we ate, and then I gave him a feed and put him down for the night.

For the rest of the evening, we sat on the patio and watched the sunset, and the stars rise. We talked about the good old days and the really great new days, as I liked to call them.

"Any news about Blaine or Eric?" Candace asked when there was a lull in the conversation.

"Nothing new," I replied, not really wanting to talk about either of them. "Eric lost his driver's license, and accepted a plea deal for reckless endangerment, which he will likely get a fine and probation. I'm pretty sure he won't be bothering us anymore unless he's gone completely insane. He has to think about his reputation, although it's been so badly tarnished, I doubt he'll be able to attract the kind of business he did before all this happened. It's his own fault for cheating on his pregnant wife."

"What a bastard," Mara said. "Why is it that really rich men can be such dicks? I mean, really poor men and men of middling means can be as well, but still. You'd think they'd be happy to be wealthy and powerful. Why lose it all over some cheap pussy? I mean, Lexxi911? Come on..."

"Don't ask me," Candace replied. "Some men are just corrupted by power. Others are corrupt to start with and become rich precisely because they have no conscience. Some men are sex addicts and can't stop, just like an alcoholic can't stop drinking or a drug addict can't stop shooting up."

Mara shook her head. "Do you really believe that sex addict BS? I always thought it was a convenient excuse to get people's sympathy. You know, 'Oh, poor me. I'm a sex addict, so I can't not go to prostitutes...' I don't believe it."

"I do," Candace said. "Some people are addicted to adrenaline. They jump out of airplanes with parachutes on their backs, or hang-glide, extreme snowboarding, mountain climbing. Their brains need the rush of endorphins, I guess, or they feel dead inside. It's the same with sex. Some people need that endorphin rush from an orgasm and become addicted. Some masturbate multiple times a day and are always paying for hookers. It's a disease."

I didn't say anything, because I honestly didn't know enough to have an opinion, but I thought that some men just took advantage of their power and wealth to do what they couldn't get away with if they were poor and were nobodies.

Give a man a million dollars, and you see what he's made of.

Luke inherited money from the death of his parents, but he also made a company through hard work and sweat. Then, he made even more when he sold *Chatter*. He was using that wealth to go to space. He was one of the good guys.

He only wanted to get married and have a loving family, and not use his money to buy women or influence.

"Speaking of wealthy men, how's Luke doing?" Mara asked. "You're the lucky one with your billionaire space dude who is happy to be a domesticated dad."

"Luke is doing fine," I said and smiled at the thought of Luke out with his hopeful investors, showing them the nightlife. "He's doing his duty to make the potential angel investors happy. That makes me happy. It's all good."

Candace smiled. "Our girl is living the dream."

I *was* living the dream and was happy to admit it. "I'm very lucky. One mistake when Luke entered Lexxi911's email address wrong and here I am. Just think — I would never have met him otherwise. Our worlds did not intersect at any point, and they wouldn't. Two different people, two different worlds."

"Fate is weird like that," Mara said.

We spent the rest of the evening reminiscing about our friendships and then when it was time, we went to our bedrooms for the night. I was so glad to have the girls with me while Luke was in town with his potential investors. While I knew there was a security detail outside watching the property, I still didn't like being alone in the beach house, so far away from everyone else.

So, it was a total shock to wake up in the middle of the night and have it not be because I needed to feed Leif.

Instead, there was a knock at my bedroom door.

"Mrs. Marshall, it's me, Gord."

I got up and pulled on my robe. I went to the door and opened it. Gord, the guard on duty that night was standing with a two-way radio in hand. A man in his forties, former military, he looked the part, with short cropped dark hair shot through with grey, and deep-set dark eyes. Tall, well over six feet tall, and heavy set. He was formidable, which made me feel safe.

"What is it?"

"We had an intruder on the property. He triggered the silent alarm, and the infrared lights, so I was able to track him without his knowledge, but he escaped and ran down the beach. I called for backup and will wait for the police to arrive."

"Oh, God," I said, shivering at the thought that someone — Blaine perhaps — had tried to come on the property, maybe to break into the house. "Do you have him on security video?"

"Yes, and if you want, you can come down to the office and check it out."

Candace popped her head out of her room, her eyes bleary. Mara followed her. "What's going on?"

"Someone came onto the property," I said and followed Gord down the hallway to the staircase. "I'm going to go look at the video."

"We're coming," she said and the two of them followed me. We went down the stairs to the main floor and then to one of the rooms in the wing of the house next to the garage. It was where the security company kept a desk and series of monitors to watch the property Gord sat down and replayed the video that showed a man wearing a hoodie climbing over the tall brick wall on the side of the property. He was outlined in green, but you couldn't see a face. There was a black ski mask hiding his facial features.

"He knew enough not to expose his face. When I came out of the side door, I called out to him as you can see here, and he ran. He jumped over the fence, using a chair from the pool, and ran down the beach. I didn't want to leave the property unprotected, so I called backup and police and let them know which way he went. Hopefully, someone will have the vehicle he came in on security cams in the area and we'll be able to find out who it was."

"I hope so," I said, but I had this sinking feeling it was Blaine, back to try to hurt me. Would he have known I'd be alone at the beach house and decided to take the opportunity to hurt me?

"Can you replay it? I want to see if I recognize the man."

"Sure," Gord said and replayed the video showing the man. I peered at the image of the man walking beside the fence but wasn't able to identify him from his body or walk.

He didn't remind me of Blaine, but it had been years since I was with him...

Whatever the case, I shivered and was glad we kept the security detail at the beach house, despite the months of no incidents since Leif was born.

Police showed up a few minutes later, and we sat down in the living room and Gord told them about the setup and what happened, while Candace and Mara sat with me and listened. The police officers then watched the video in the office, and one of them explored the property. While we watched, Gord showed the officer where the intruder had breached the wall and how he had escaped.

I heard a cry from Leif's bedroom and went upstairs to find him wiggling under his blanket, ready for his feeding.

I picked him up and his diaper was sopping, so I changed him and then sat in the rocking chair, the night-light shining stars and a large moon on the ceiling above us. He nursed eagerly, but after a while, when he was almost full, his little eyes closed, and he fell asleep at the breast. I

S. E. LUND

smiled to myself, and put him on my shoulder for a burp, which he delivered almost right away. Despite all the turmoil of the evening, he would be able to sleep soundly, even if his mother and his two adoptive aunties had the creeps because of the attempted break-in.

Had the man planned to break into the house and hurt us? Hurt me?

I shivered after I put Leif back into his crib, and then closed the door behind me. I was glad the nursery was on the second floor. Leif was safe at least.

I went back to the living room where Mara and Candace were still sitting, drinking cups of hot tea.

"You two not going back to bed?"

"Aren't you going to call Luke and let him know what happened?"

"Should I?" I plopped down beside Candace. "What good will it do? It will just ruin his one chance at sleeping through the night.

Then, my cell rang, and I checked. It was Luke.

"Hey, babe," I said. "Did Gord call you? I didn't want to wake you up, since we're all okay."

"Yes, he did. And I'm glad he did. Are you okay?"

"I'm fine. Leif just had his feed and is now asleep. Candace and Mara and I are trying to decompress before going back to bed."

"I'm coming home right now."

"Don't you dare! You go back to bed and sleep in. No need. I have the girls here and Gord is with us. Stay. Have breakfast in the room. You love their Big Breakfast..."

"I'm on my way. You go back to bed, and I'll see you when I get home."

"Luke..."

"I'm not taking no for an answer. I wouldn't be able to

48

enjoy the Big Breakfast, knowing what happened. See you soon."

With that, he ended the call and I sighed and turned to Mara and Candace. "He's coming home."

"Aww, what a sweetheart," Candace said. "He really loves you two."

I smiled and nodded in agreement. He really did.

I was a lucky lucky woman.

CHAPTER 7

Luke

THE DRIVE OUT TO THE BEACH HOUSE WAS FASTER THAN normal due to the light traffic in the middle of the night, and we made record time. When the limo stopped at the front entrance, I grabbed my overnight bag and briefcase and thanked the driver, gave him an extra fifty as a tip, and went inside. The lights were all on, but the only people on the main floor were Gord and a police officer, who were in the office by the garage, watching security footage.

"Hey, Gord," I said and went to shake his hand. He introduced me to the police officer who was handling the prowler report, Officer Rob Jennings. An older cop with a shaved head, he had a very serious expression on his beefy face, and light blue eyes that seemed suspicious. I figured he would do well in an interrogation.

The three of us sat at the desk and watched the video replay, so Gord could walk me through what happened.

"Mrs. Marshall told me that there are two people in particular that you are concerned with," Jennings said.

"Yes," I replied and went on to describe Blaine, who he was to us, and what he'd tried to do to hurt Alexa before.

I watched the video of the man who jumped the fence, but he seemed younger than Blaine, who was in his thirties. The person who jumped the fence appeared to be in his early twenties.

"It might have just been a prowler, looking for something to steal," I said, and shrugged. "Blaine is older and heavier set, at least from what I saw of him in photos."

"Could be. The houses along the beach are very expensive, but they all have top of the line security in place, so this guy wasn't very smart to try to break in."

"Aren't most criminals on the dumb side?" Gord asked.

"Yeah, the run of the mill kind," Jennings replied. "Hardened career criminals are pretty savvy. This guy knew to cover his face so we wouldn't be able to use facial recognition software, so he wasn't too dumb."

We talked for another twenty minutes, and then when Officer Jennings was satisfied, he said goodbye and left the house. I thanked Gord once more and heading upstairs. I popped my head into Leif's nursery and saw that he was sleeping soundly. Part of me wanted to pick him up and hold him, to reassure myself that he was okay, but the other part realized that if I did, he might wake up and demand a feed.

I satisfied myself by adjusting the baby blanket covering him and I watched him for a moment, glad that he was fine.

I left the nursery, closing the door carefully so I didn't wake him and then I went to the master suite.

When I opened the door, I saw that Alexa was asleep, her hands folded under her chin, her eyes closed. She must have fallen asleep with the relaxation tape playing, for there were ear buds still in her ears. I smiled, and undressed, then crept in beside her, trying my best not to wake her up. Thankfully, she didn't, probably being exhausted by the middle of the night chaos of the prowler and the police report.

I lay in bed, my eyes wide open, and stared at the ceiling, watching as the thin sliver of light from between the curtains at the window crept across the wall. I thought about how lucky I was to have the life I had, the beautiful smart loving wife, the healthy baby boy, and felt a stab of fear that there were people out there who wanted to hurt them.

Sleep was a long time in coming.

I WOKE the next morning to the sound of the water running in the master bathroom. I glanced at my watch and saw that it was already eight thirty, and Alexa was up having a shower. My morning wood was a reminder that I hadn't had sex since the last time Alexa and I were on one of our weekends away, care of Mr. and Mrs. Dixon. I felt like sneaking into the shower with Alexa and hoping that she felt like a quickie, but I didn't want to make her feel guilty and go along with me, despite not feeling like it.

Instead of getting up as I would have liked, I stayed in bed with the pillow over my head and decided to wait for my own shower to take care of business.

I wanted Alexa to want me as much as I wanted her, and I could wait — happily — until she felt that way. Our first few sessions of making love had been entirely voluntary on her part and I wanted it to stay that way. I always felt like it, but I knew that her body had been taxed to the limit by motherhood and nursing. I couldn't expect her to want it as much as I did, or even as much as she used to.

Not for a while, at least.

I heard the shower end, and then after a while, Alexa came back into our bedroom, and I heard her opening the closet doors to select her clothes for the day. She definitely was trying not to wake me, and so I didn't move or indicate that I was awake.

Then, I felt bad. I didn't want anything to come between us, and pretending I was asleep felt like I was deceiving her, even if it was because I didn't want to make her feel like she had to deal with me.

So, I turned over and took the pillow from over top of my head and put it under it instead.

"Hey, Mrs. Marshall. How are you feeling today? Did you sleep well enough?"

She turned to face me as she pulled on her sundress, her smile making me feel like I'd done the right thing.

"I'm fine, Mr. Marshall, and I did have a decent sleep, all things considered." She finished zipping up her sundress and then came over to the bed and climbed on beside me, bending down over me, her arms on either side of my shoulders. "Do you have a kiss for your wife?"

I covered my mouth with a hand. "You can kiss me on the forehead, if you want," I mumbled. "You'll have to wait for a proper kiss until after I brush my own teeth."

She grinned and did just that, kissing my forehead and then both cheeks, one after the other.

"We have a date weekend coming up," she said. "If you can hold out until then, I'm sure we'll be able to enjoy ourselves properly. I miss you..."

"I'm yours," I said and pulled her into my arms. "Anytime you want me." She laid her head on my shoulder and we enjoyed the warmth of each other's embrace for a moment.

Of course, a snuffling sound came over the baby monitor on the bedside table.

"Duty calls," Alexa said and winked at me. She kissed be quickly on the mouth before I could cover it again and then left the bed, sprinting to the bedroom door.

I sighed in contentment, glad that she was beginning to feel a need for us to connect once more the way we did before Leif came along.

Her libido was recovering, in other words...

I got up and had a quick shower, then after brushing my teeth and giving my stubble a bit of a shave, I got dressed and went to the nursery to see if they were there.

Alexa must have already changed Leif and taken him downstairs for a feed, so I went to the main floor. Sure enough, she sat at the kitchen island with Candace and Mara on either side of her, Leif at her breast.

"There she is," I said and kissed her, then kissed the baldish head of my son. "My two favorite people in the entire world."

I caught Candace's smile at my words and turned to give her and Mara my attention. "I'm so glad you two were here with Alexa, considering what happened last night. How are you doing? Were you able to sleep afterwards?"

"Like a baby," Candace said. "It's amazing what having a security guard on duty will do to your sense of safety."

"Me too," Mara said with a nod. "Slept like the proverbial baby."

"How was your meeting with the prospective investors?" Alexa asked, turning her attention to me.

I went to the kitchen counter and poured myself a cup

of coffee. "Fine," I said and described the evening. "I got to meet my future partners, so it was a good night all around."

I sat down beside Candace and drank my coffee, while she and Mara took turns telling me about the previous night's events. Alexa listened, adding in a comment or two.

"I'm glad you two were here," I said again. "While I have full confidence in Gord and the security company to protect us, I'm sure Alexa was glad to have you both here to help her deal with it."

"We're glad, too," Candace said. "Plus, we got to spend more time with Leif and experience what it's like to have to get up in the middle of the night to feed a baby."

"Don't let it put you off having one yourself," I said, but couldn't hold back a yawn. "You get used to the interrupted sleep after several months. Or so they tell me..."

We all laughed at that.

"Sure," Alexa said with a grin. "Tell me another one, Daddy."

"All right, all right," I said and grinned back. "You learn to tolerate the interrupted sleep, especially when you're holding the little man in your arms, and he smiles up at you."

"Aww," Candace said and made a pouty face. "That's just so sweet."

"It's true," Alexa said. "You can be really tired, and wishing that Leif would sleep through the night, but then, I'm holding him, and he smiles and that does it. Putty in his hands."

"I swear that a baby's smile is evolution's way of making us fall in love with our babies, so we keep feeding them even in the middle of the night when we're zonked," Mara added.

We all laughed at that, and I watched Alexa holding Leif and him struggling to keep his eyes open. He often fell asleep at the breast, and it was always funny when he'd wake up once Alexa put him on her shoulder for a burp.

Which he proceeded to do for us, his little squeak of upset at being woken making me smile all over again.

"I can do that if you want," I offered. I grabbed a clean diaper off the countertop and placed it on my shoulder, then held my arms out. "Let me burp him. I've been away."

"Okay, Daddy," Alexa said and handed Leif over. I took him in my arms and placed him onto my shoulder. His little back arched and he complained but soon, a big burp erupted, and we all laughed at how big it was, considering his small size.

Life was good.

I felt that, even though we'd had the scare of someone trespassing on the property, things were looking up for us. Elena and Jack seemed really committed to investing in Astra-Seneca, Alexa and I were reigniting the sexual part of our relationship and Leif was a healthy happy baby.

I hoped it would stay that way.

CHAPTER 8

Alexa

FOR THE NEXT WEEK, LUKE AND I SPENT MOST OF OUR time with Leif, taking long walks along the beach, and spending our evenings on the patio, enjoying the last warmth of the summer. It was cooler along the coast, so we didn't suffer too much from the hot days, and I kept the window open at night so I could hear the sound of the surf in the distance.

It was calming, and I loved to smell the salt air.

Police had done some canvasing of the neighborhood to see if anyone's Ring camera caught the prowler who had scaled the wall around our property, but so far, there was nothing solid to identify who it was. Police wondered if the man didn't have a boat somewhere and escaped that way. There were literally dozens of small piers and boat launch areas along the coast near the beach house that someone could moor their boat, and then escape if they wanted to.

Some of the houses had security cameras pointed towards the beach, but none observed a boat taking off around the time of the prowler, so we had no luck on that side either. Whoever it was, they escaped being caught and that left me with an uneasy feeling that we were not safe, even with all the security surrounding us.

I should have realized that security had worked exactly the way it was supposed to. The prowler was detected by the security system, and Gord had been alerted and had gone to chase him down. I hoped it was just a local break-in artist who was looking for valuables and not Blaine or Eric hoping to get revenge, but I didn't know for sure.

As long as there was a possibility it had been either of them — or someone they hired to do the job — I would feel uncertain and unsafe.

I didn't want to reveal my fears to Luke, because he had done everything in his power to protect us, and it was costing a lot of money to keep security at the level it was at, with monitoring of the property, the patrol of the area by a guard in a vehicle, a guard on duty at all times. But it was worth it.

One day, I hoped we could end it but until Eric and Blaine were either in jail or dead, I feared it wouldn't.

I WENT into the office and found Luke sitting at his desk, his back to the door. He was wearing a crisp white shirt and tie but was still wearing his boxer briefs. He had ear buds in and was conducting a Zoom meeting with John and some other people — one of them a very beautiful woman with dark hair and eyes. They were all smiling and laughing at something, so I popped out of the office, feeling bad that I interrupted a business meeting.

I went into the living room and tried to enjoy some alone time while Leif was sleeping, grabbing the iPad and reading some headlines while Luke was in his meeting. I had grown used to having him around me all the time, and had forgotten that he was still a businessman, still had to conduct his business at least part-time, and that he wasn't mine 24/7. About an hour later, he emerged from the office and removed the earbuds.

"Hey," he said and plopped down beside me on the sofa. "Leif still asleep? That's long for him."

"He was fussy in the night, so I guess he's making up for lost sleep." I turned to him. "Sorry about popping into the office like that while you were in the middle of a Zoom meeting. I forgot you have a real life outside of being a new dad."

"No problem, he said and leaned over to kiss me. "I didn't even notice and I'm sure my colleagues didn't either. The camera is zoomed in on me, so they must not have seen you come in. They wouldn't be upset even if they did. They know the score."

"Do they?"

"They do," I said. "I told them before the meeting that I might be called away at any time by a crying baby and to be prepared just in case. They understand, and if they don't, too bad for them."

Luke smiled and folded his arms like that was that.

I leaned over and kissed him back. "You're a great dad to do this, you know."

Luke sighed wistfully. "I wish I'd had a dad who was willing to stay home with me when I was a baby and look after me along with my mom, but it just wasn't done back in the day. Parental leave was just not a thing. So glad that's different."

He peered at my iPad and at the crossword I was doing. "How's the crossword?"

For the next half hour while Leif still slept without waking, we did the crossword together. Luke got up and made us both a fresh cup of coffee and then, when the crossword was done, we did the Wordle.

Almost two hours after Leif went down for his nap, a faint cry came over the baby monitor, signalling that he was waking up.

"That's Leif," Luke said and jumped up. "I'll go get him."

"I can do it," I said, getting up as well. I checked my watch. "You should go and either get fully dressed or go for a run."

"No, I got this," Luke said and shook his head. "I want some baby daddy time."

I smiled and watched Luke leave for the second floor and Leif's bedroom.

While Luke changed Leif, I went to the kitchen and cleaned up a bit, deciding on what we'd have for lunch. Outside, the sun was shining through a break in the clouds, and it looked like a really nice day was brewing. A walk along the beach with Leif in a stroller would be a nice way to spend the afternoon.

I heard Luke talking to Leif while I organized the pantry and listened as Leif snuffled and cried.

That didn't sound like his usual bubbly baby talk. In fact, Leif sounded all stuffed up.

A small bit of concern filled me that he was sick, but I tried to damp that down by reminding myself that babies got a lot of colds. Leif had already taken his first vaccines, and we'd been lucky that he hadn't been sick yet. I knew it would happen eventually, but still was worried.

Finally, Luke came down the stairs with Leif in his arms. Luke was frowning, and so my fears were justified.

"I think he's hot," Luke said and pressed his lips against Leif's forehead. "You should get the thermometer."

"Okay," I said. "Does he have the sniffles?"

"He's snorting a bit," Luke replied. "He's grousing a bit, too."

"Okay." I went to the main floor bathroom and retrieved the ear thermometer that we had in the drawer and sat beside Luke on the sofa. Leif was lying on his lap and so I turned on the thermometer and held it inside Leif's ear until I heard the beep.

Sure enough, his temperature was raised.

"Yes," I said and showed Luke. "It's 100.5"

"What do we do?"

"We call the doctor and see what she says."

I grabbed my cell and called Leif's paediatrician, who we registered with even before Leif was born. I spoke with the receptionist and told her about Leif's temperature and sniffles. "Can you get the doctor to call me? Let me know what we should do?"

"She'll call you as soon as she has a break between patients."

"Thanks," I said and ended the call. I turned to Luke. "She'll call during a break."

"Okay," Luke said. "I'm sure it's nothing. Just a cold. Babies get fevers when they get a virus, so I'm sure if we give him some acetaminophen, he'll be fine. Just like the baby book says."

I nodded, but of course, I was nervous. This was our

first sickness, and I wanted to handle it like a grown up, but inside I felt afraid.

Once that was done, Luke handed Leif to me and I gave him the breast, which he took happily, snuffling away while he drank with difficulty, but managing to get a decent feed in. Finally, the feeding over, and Leif on Luke's shoulder for a burp, the doctor called, the number for the office showing up on my cell's call display.

"Hello, Dr. Anderson? Thanks for calling."

I told her about Leif's temperature, and how he was stuffy and had some difficulty nursing, and she reassured us that it was common for babies to get a virus, probably brought into the house by an asymptomatic friend or family member.

"You need to keep him well hydrated and use the nasal syringe to remove any secretions regularly, so he can breathe more easily. Give him some acetaminophen as per the dosage on the package and watch him for the next couple of days. If he doesn't improve, if he shows no interest in feeding, or if his fever doesn't go away within say, forty-eight hours, call and make an appointment."

"Thanks, Doctor Anderson," I said. "We will."

I ended the call and glanced at Luke, who was patting Leif's back. "Well, we have a couple of days to wait and see how Leif does."

"Okay. I'm sure he'll be fine." Luke smiled at me encouragingly. Of course, I wasn't as optimistic as he was. I always seemed to fear the worst.

Luke handed Leif back to me and I held him, looking up his tiny nostrils to see if they were plugged. "She said to give him acetaminophen and get the nasal syringe and clean out mucus. Can you get it for me?"

Luke went to the bathroom and retrieved the acetaminophen bottle and the red rubber bulb with the hole at the end.

"I saw it demonstrated on that baby care video," Luke said and squeezed the bulb several times. "You insert the end into the nostril when it's depressed just a bit and then let it inflate. It sucks the mucus out."

I measured out the acetaminophen and gave it to Leif. He sucked away at the syringe, apparently enjoying the sweet taste. When that was done, I examined the red nasal bulb. "You want to do it?" I asked, making a face.

"Sure," Luke said. He laid Leif on his lap with his head on Luke's knees. Luke practiced it a couple of times and then nodded. "Okay. Here goes." I watched, nervous, as Luke deflated the bulb a tiny bit and then inserted the very tip of the bulb into Leif's left nostril. Leif squirmed and Luke was able to inflate the bulb, successfully removing some snot from it.

"Voila!" Luke held up the bulb and smiled at me. "Piece of cake." He squeezed the mucus out onto a tissue and then did it again just to make sure he removed more of the material. He repeated this with the other nostril and soon, little Leif was breathing a bit easier.

"Success," Luke said with a grin. "It's not hard. You should try the next time. Just in case you need to do it, and I'm not here for some reason."

"Okay," I said and took in a deep breath. "I'll do it the next time."

We sat and watched Leif as he wiggled on Luke's lap, smiling at the toy Luke held up in front of his face.

It would be a tense couple of days while we watched to see how Leif did with whatever virus was making him sick. Hopefully, it was just a cold and would pass in a few days. The most we would have to do was clean out his nose

S. E. LUND

frequently, give him his regular dose of acetaminophen, and make sure his temperature was under control.

I laid my head on Luke's shoulder and tried to enjoy our time together.

Within an hour, I took Leif's temperature again and it was indeed down and was now only 99.4. Almost normal. Hopefully, that would be the most it would be if we kept the level of acetaminophen up in his blood and he would be better in a day or two.

Whatever the case, my idea of a nice walk along the beach in the afternoon was out. I didn't want to make Leif either too hot or too cold, considering.

I was glad Luke was at home with me. I didn't like the idea of being solely responsible for Leif while he was sick and once more, I realized how lucky I was to have Luke.

"I'm glad you're at home with me," I said as I changed Leif and to get him ready for his afternoon nap. "I'd be really nervous if I had to deal with this alone. I honestly don't know how mothers did it all by themselves all these years."

"I'm glad to be here dealing with this with you," Luke said, standing at my side at the change table, watching while I put on a clean onesie. "In fact, I couldn't stand not being here while he's sick. I'd be unable to concentrate on work if I thought you were here all by yourself." He shook his head. "It's really criminal that every man doesn't have parental leave rights in this country, considering how wealthy we are as a nation."

"Agreed," I said. I kissed Leif on the head and then held him out so Luke could do the same. Then, I laid him in his crib and turned on the mobile so that a soft lullaby played, and the stuffed rockets and stars paraded around above him.

He seemed really entranced with the sound and sight of

the mobile, and Luke and I were able to sneak out of the room. We watched from the doorway as Leif wiggled a bit but eventually settled down.

We were lucky to have such an easy baby and we knew it. Many parents had babies that were fussy, colicky, or had other digestive issues. Leif was easy, not fussy and seemed to go to sleep pretty well without much effort. He did wake in the night for a feed or two, but that was it.

We were blessed.

CHAPTER 9

Luke

Despite Leif's sniffles, he slept well enough and only woke for one feed.

Alexa woke up at four in the morning and sat up in bed.

"Did you hear him cry?"

I stretched. "No."

We both listened to the monitor on the bedside table, but there was no sound. "He's sleeping," I said and picked it up so I could show Alexa the image on the video monitor. "Look. You can see his chest moving. He's sleeping soundly. He's fine."

Alexa nodded, but I could tell she was still concerned. "I'm worried that he's really sick if he hasn't even woken up twice to feed."

"Try to sleep," I said and put my arms around her after she lay back down in bed. She finally snuggled into my arms and for a while, we both listened to the baby monitor. "We have to take advantage of this and get a good sleep if Leif is going to. Besides, he's breathing fine, and his fever seems down."

"It always goes down in the night, plus he took Tylenol, so that brought it down. Whatever's making him sick is still there."

"Shh," I said and turned off the nightlight. "Try to relax. We'll see how he is in the morning."

Finally, she must have relaxed since she fell asleep.

On the other hand, I lay awake for quite a while, listening to her breathing, and the occasional sniff coming from the baby monitor. I suddenly felt the immensity of my responsibilities for Alexa and now Leif. There was a lot going on at the time regarding our quest to get funding for our venture, and my mind was whirling trying to keep track of everything on my to-do list. Even though I was on parental leave, I still made it into the office several times a week just to catch up with what was going on and to meet with John or whoever I needed to so I could keep on top of things. But my focus during the first six months of Leif's life was raising him and being the best dad that I could be and the best partner to Alexa.

Still as hard as I tried to keep my focus on my home life, my mind frequently wandered to the office. I felt guilty at times that I wasn't properly focused on house and home and my role as Leif's father. Luckily, Alexa understood. She told me to go into the city twice a week just to keep track of things and that I shouldn't feel bad.

She was doing fine, and she promised that if she needed help, she could call her mother, who had lots of information and knowledge from raising Alexa.

Of course, that just made me feel worse. I should have been able to focus on our home life and our baby and put the business aside. It would still be there when Leif was a year old.

So, I was glad that Alexa gave me permission to go into the city at least twice a week for a few hours. She didn't mind being alone with Leif. I still felt guilty leaving but took Alexa at her word that she'd be fine.

THE NEXT MORNING, I was scheduled to go into town and meet with John to discuss prospects for new angel investors coming on to the project. While both Alexa and Leif slept, I had a quick shower and got ready to go into work. I watched from my closet while Alexa slept in our bed, her hands tucked beside her face, her eyes closed. Luckily Leif slept in and so Alexa got a few more hours of sleep.

I went over to the bed and bent down to give Alexa a kiss. In response, she snuggled down and smiled when she felt my lips on her cheek.

"You going in already? What time is it?" she asked.

"It's 6:30," I said. "I'll make you a pot of coffee before I go."

She smiled and snuggled down even more deeply into the comforter. "I love you," she said. I kissed her again. "I love you, too," I replied, smiling to myself.

I left the bedroom and passed by the nursery. I gingerly opened the door and peeked inside. Leif was still asleep, his little hands clenched into fists, his head turned to the side. The room was dim, but there was a glow from the star globe on the walls and ceilings. I closed the door quietly, careful not to make a sound, and then went downstairs to the kitchen. I made a fresh pot of coffee, poured myself one into my travel thermos, and then called down for my ride.

I told the driver that I'd be ready in five, and he said he would pull into the driveway and wait. I gathered my brief-case and my files, and then went to the door to get my jacket and shoes. I turned to take one last look at the house and realized that I'd forgotten the coffee mug, so I went back and retrieved it from the counter.

The view from the patio doors was magnificent and I felt bad that I would be missing the morning with Alexa and Leif. I consoled myself that there would be many more mornings like this one that we could spend together. The success of Astra Investments depended on getting enough funding so that we could fulfill our promises to our investors. That meant I had to be on top of things and so I had to leave my wonderful wife and beautiful son at least twice a week, but it was a price I was willing to pay.

I left the house and got into the back of the limo. After saying hello to the driver, I opened my laptop and spent the drive into town catching up on the latest investment news. I checked out my own investments to see how they were doing, and everything was going well all things considered. At least Alexa, Leif and I wouldn't have to worry about our own finances. Our needs would be taken care of even if Astra Investments didn't do as well as I hoped.

Once we arrived in the city, I went up to the penthouse and into my office. I said hello to my admin assistant, Karl, and then sat down behind my desk. I checked my inbox for mail and messages and saw that it was coming up to 9 and my first meeting with John.

I grabbed my file, refilled my coffee in the break room, and then went to John's office. I popped my head inside and saw that he was on the phone. I pointed to the boardroom and mouthed *See you in 5*. He nodded and so I left his office and went down the hall to the boardroom where we were supposed to meet.

After getting seated and organizing my materials on the desktop in front of me, I checked my phone to see if Alexa had texted. Sure enough, there was a text from her and a picture of her holding Leif and sitting on the patio. She was smiling and Leif looked happy with his pacifier in his mouth.

ALEXA: We are living our best life out here on the patio. Love you. OXOX.

I smiled and sent back a text.

LUKE: I wish I was with you, instead of in this board-room waiting to meet with John. Will have the rest of the season together. Love you. Give Leif a kiss and hug for me.

John finally arrived, and we spent the next hour going over business relating to Astra Investments, especially a new investor who wanted to join the consortium, Frank Campbell of Campbell Investments, Inc.

"I spoke with Frank, and he thinks we should move our headquarters to Austin, TX, as soon as possible. There's a lot of work being done in the aerospace industry and related technology. He thinks we should be there so we can meet with others in the industry. Meet our competition."

"I don't know," I said and frowned. "I always thought we'd keep our headquarters in New York and have subsidiary offices in Texas and California. That would workout best for me because of Alexa's university and job prospects."

"Isn't she almost done?" John asked. "She's finishing her PhD, right?"

"Yes, she's almost done, but she also wants to work in her field, which is primarily located in New York, Washington DC, or in European capitals."

S. E. LUND

"Campbell Investments is a big deal," John replied, his eyes wide. "I thought you understood. Campbell's investment would mean we could really start competing, and he wants to see us move to either California or Texas, but Austin is his number one location. I don't think we can accept his money if we aren't willing to go along with his ideas. He has a lot of experience in the aerospace industry."

I sighed heavily. Of course, John was right, and Campbell Investments was a very big deal. In fact, it was such a big deal that it could mean the difference between lingering in obscurity as an aerospace company or hitting the big times and competing directly with other aerospace businesses like SpaceX. However, the prospect of moving family to Austin TX was not a happy one.

"I'll have to talk to Alexa about this, but I'm I not sure she'll like the idea."

John frowned. "You're wealthy enough that she could fly anywhere she wanted at any time at the drop of a hat," John said. "You could have a house in Austin, a house in New York or Brussels or wherever, and still run the business out of Texas."

I rubbed my chin and considered. Of course, John was right, and I was wealthy enough to have houses in multiple cities, but where would our home be located? That was what mattered. I wanted somewhere stable for Leif to grow up. I wanted to feel some sense of community where we lived. I wanted a good school, a good neighborhood, and a good environment for Leif to grow up in, and I wasn't sure about Texas.

"I'll talk to Alexa," I said. "I know she'd like to stay in New York, and even talked about us relocating to somewhere in Europe, depending on where she gets a job, but that's a few years off anyway. Let's just say we'll play it by ear for now. See what Campbell really wants and what his bottom line is. When are we meeting with him?"

"This Saturday," John replied. "I hope you'll be there, and I hope that you and Alexa can attend the dinner and drinks afterward. Maybe you guys could stay in town and hire a babysitter for Leif so you can spend time with Campbell. I know he wants to meet with you and get a sense of who you are. He'd like to meet Alexa, too, I'm sure."

"Of course, we will," I said. "Of course, we can stay at the apartment, and get a sitter. Alexa will probably enjoy a night out."

"Good," John said and shuffled some papers. "It's settled. The meeting is Saturday afternoon here, and then dinner and drinks with all our new investors."

I nodded in reply, but a part of me didn't like the prospect of deciding where to locate our head offices. I put it to the back of my mind. We had to secure the funding before moving our head office anywhere.

For the next hour, John and I went over the latest business numbers and statistics, and then I went back to my office when the meeting was done to get some work finished, because I only planned to stay the morning.

It was then that Elena Marakova knocked on my door. She popped her head in the office and smiled when our eyes met. I was surprised to see her in the office, and didn't expect to see her, but she and Jack must have been in the city for the week.

"Elena," I said and sat up, closing the file on my desk. "I didn't know you were still in city. Come in and have a seat. What can I do for you?"

She came in the office and closed the door behind her. "I decided to stay in town for the week, since we're meeting on Saturday. I decided that some extra time spent here would be good, given some of the more recent developments." She took the seat across from my desk crossing her legs and adjusting her jacket. She ran after hand through her hair and then licked her lips. I had the distinct sense that she was trying to appear attractive to me.

"New developments? John didn't say anything to me I our meeting this morning."

"I haven't had the time to speak with him yet. I knew you were coming in today, and I wanted to be here so we could chat. How is your little wife doing? And your baby-what was his name Lee?"

"Leif," I said. "Like Leif Erickson. You know, the Viking explorer."

"You named your child after a Viking?"

I laughed. "Alexa and I are big fans of Vikings, the TV show. Plus, I have some Norwegian blood in me, and we thought it would be fun to name him something appropriate. As to Alexa, she's doing fine," I said, irritated with Elena's reference to Alexa as *'your little wife.'* That was something I would expect from a boomer, not someone of my own generation, but perhaps Elena didn't have a high opinion of motherhood.

I folded my hands. "Speaking of families, when are you getting married? Do you plan to have any children?"

Elena brushed her hair back. "If I do get married," she said. "It will be only after I've secured my business future, not before. That ruined my mother's career chances, pregnancy and marriage, and I won't let it ruin mine."

I shrugged. "I don't plan on letting it ruin Alexis prospects."

She adjusted her position. "Employers don't look favorably at gaps in employment history," she said, straightening her back. "You should make sure to tell Alexa that she should postpone working until she can make sure she doesn't have to take a break because of the baby. That's looked on as worse than taking a long gap after pregnancy and then returning to work full time. Prospective employers want to see commitment to the job and to the career, and don't care about family. I know this from experience and have heard HR professionals talk about when to hire women and when not to. My mother and my sister both suffered because they got pregnant and married." She shrugged. "Just offering some friendly advice."

"Well, thank you for your advice," I said, slightly irritated with her attitude. "I'm sure everything will work out fine for Alexa and for Leif. I'll make sure it does."

"Good luck," Elena said. "You'll need it. Alexa will need it.

I sighed and checked my watch. "Was there anything else? I thought you said there were important developments." I said, even more irritated. I reopened the file on my desktop to signal that on my part, the meeting was over.

"Yes, actually," Elena said and stood up. "I don't want to spill the beans, so to speak, until we can get together, the four of us. Jack wants us to meet for lunch and we wanted to make sure you and John attend since you're both principals."

I hesitated. I had planned on returning to the beach house as soon as my meetings were over so I could spend the afternoon with Alexa and Leif. I didn't want to change plans, but at the same time, I knew it would be important to attend the lunch since Elena hinted there were important new developments Jack wanted to discuss.

"We can't meet here before lunch? It's still only 11:30."

"Unfortunately, Jack is in another meeting and can't make it until 12:30 so he asked if we could meet him at the restaurant instead of him coming here. Kill two birds with one stone, so to speak."

"Fine," I said. "I'll have to change plans, but I can attend. Text me when you're ready to go, and I'll meet you in the lobby."

"Good, good," Elena said. "I know that Jack really wants to get together with you and John to discuss this very exciting news. There's lots going on behind the scenes that we haven't been able to tell you about. Really exciting developments. I'll text you when it's time."

"Sounds good," I said and gave her a smile. "I'll see you later."

Elena stood and adjusted her skirt, and then smiled at me. "I look forward to it."

Then she left the office, closing the door behind her. I exhaled heavily, feeling bad that I was going to change plans and not go home for lunch with Alexa. I took out my cell phone and sent Alexa a text to let her know that I would be home mid-afternoon and would miss having lunch with her and Leif.

I hope she understood.

She texted right back.

ALEXA: Of course, I understand you have to stay for the business lunch meeting. Exciting new developments? I can't wait to hear the details. Leif and I will be fine on our own. See you when you get here. Love you. XOXO

I smiled at the text and sent her a few XOs back.

Then, I texted John.

LUKE: What do you know about this mystery meeting with Jack and Elena? Any deets at all?

John texted me back.

JOHN: Not yet. I'm as in the dark as you are. See you downstairs. We can take the limo together.

I texted him back and then checked my watch, a sense of excitement growing about the meeting with Jack.

I hoped it was really great news, like a big investor coming on board.

If so, I would pick up a nice bottle of non-alcoholic champagne so Alexa and I could celebrate at the beach house.

CHAPTER 10

Alexa

Luke's text showed up at about 11:30.

I had just finished feeding Leif and had put him down for a nap. I was thinking about what to prepare for lunch. There was leftover lasagna from the previous evening that Luke had made, trying out a new recipe he found in a vegetarian magazine he discovered on the internet. We decided to go vegetarian two days a week, for health reasons and to do our part in reducing greenhouse gasses.

We also had lots of eggs, bacon and even some frozen hash browns in the freezer that I could whip up into a nice brunch. It all depended on how Luke felt. I intended to message him and ask what he wanted but he beat me to it.

I had to admit I was a little upset that he wouldn't be coming home for lunch, but I understood that he needed to stay and deal with the investors. Business before pleasure had always been Luke's motto, and I didn't want to be a bad influence on him.

I had to trust that he knew what was necessary to run the business profitably.

Leif was sleeping soundly at the moment, and based on his usual schedule, he'd be down for at least another half hour. I was sitting on the patio looking out at the ocean. Since I was going to be alone, I decided to have a poached egg on toast and some orange juice instead of going to any trouble since Luke wouldn't be there.

My cell phone chimed, indicating an incoming text or email and for a moment, I thought it might be Luke saying that plans had changed once more and that he would be out for lunch after all, but I was wrong. Instead, it was an email from Professor Helen Turner, who taught me international relations during my master's degree and with whom I had a very good relationship.

Dear Alexa,

I hope this email find you well. I was just appointed to a position in Brussels working for the International Committee on Peace and Reconciliation, an independent agency of the European Parliament. I was hoping to hire you as my executive assistant and as a policy advisor. I know you're not finished your dissertation yet, but you could work on it part time and work for me. This is a great opportunity for me, and I want the best people to work with me in the office there. I'm sure the experience would be great for your dissertation. You would get to see the inside workings of the international peacekeeping effort.

I realize you just had a baby, so we would make sure to have childcare available for you on site and flexible work hours, sick leave, etc. That way you wouldn't have to worry about motherhood. I know Luke is involved in the aerospace industry, and the European Space Agency is located nearby in Paris. Luke could become involved with them if that interested him or was appropriate. The aerospace industry is booming in Europe.

Let me know if you're interested by next week, Monday at the latest if possible, and we can meet to discuss. I realize this is probably sooner than you hoped, given your new baby and dissertation work, but I could think of no one else I wanted to work with than you.

I read her email over several times my pulse thrumming with excitement.

Of course, I wanted to go and work with her in Brussels, Belgium. It had been my dream ever since I started studying international relations to work either at the UN or in Europe in some capacity. Brussels was second only to New York City, where the UN was located.

At the same time, I knew that Luke wasn't going to like the idea of moving to Belgium. While it was true that the European Space Agency was located in Paris, Luke was an entrepreneur, not a technician or scientist. He wanted to develop a commercial space venture that would go to the asteroid belt and mine it for rare minerals that were becoming scarce here on earth and would be key to a switch to carbon neutral energy, such as solar. Plus, all our electronics relied on these rare minerals that were getting rarer by the month as demand surged.

The places he most wanted to be included California or Florida, where there were frequent launches. The European Space agency did launch from French Guiana, located in South America, but there were several locations in the continental US where private ventures could launch.

Luke definitely wanted to stay in the States.

We had discussed it before and had decided to wait and

see what opportunities arose and that we would decide together. My PhD wasn't finished and so I figured I would adjust my career around whatever happened with Astra Investments.

No matter what, Luke assured me that we would do everything in our power to compromise so that both of us were fulfilled.

"I don't want you sacrificing any of your dreams for me," Luke said to me when we agreed to get married.

"And I don't want you to sacrifice your dreams for me," I replied, slipping on the ring he'd given me.

We both meant it, but would Luke be happy leaving the USA behind? He could always fly to the US for important meetings, and could do the rest over Zoom or Skype, but would that be enough contact?

I wasn't sure. All I knew was that this offer from Dr. Turner was like a dream come true for me.

I had to consider it seriously.

I called Candace.

"Hey, kiddo. How's the kiddo?" she said, amusement in her voice.

"Leif is fine. He's down for a nap."

"What's up?"

I sighed heavily. "I just got a job offer from a former prof who has been appointed to the International Committee on Peace and Reconciliation and wants to hire me as an EA and policy advisor. It's located in Brussels."

"Oh, geez...I suppose that means you'd have to move to Belgium. I don't know if I like that idea. Bad move."

"Why?"

"Well, for one, I would rarely get to see you guys..." She made a sniffing sound.

"You think it's a bad move?"

She burst out laughing. "Are you kidding? You gotta do it, girl! Brussels, Belgium? Come on… That's been a dream of yours since we met. You gotta go."

"What about Luke?"

"He's rich as sin and could fly back to the US whenever he wanted, first class, and write it off as a business expense. You could hire a full-time nanny and housekeeper. It sounds like a dream."

I sighed. "You think?"

"I think," she said firmly. "I think you'd be nuts if you don't say yes."

"I have to talk to Luke first. He's got his own plans for Astra Investments."

"Plans that could be carried out from anywhere in the world. There is a whole business model that developed to serve the needs of rich investment types who need to travel around the world to carry out their plans. Sure, you two would be apart for some of the time, but you'd adjust. Leif would adjust. It could work. You two have to make it work. This is your dream, girl. You didn't even have to chase it. It found you. I'd say that's a gift. It's karma."

I chewed a fingernail, unsure of what to do. "I have to talk to Luke and my parents. They've been really helpful since Leif was born. I'm sure they'd be upset if we moved to Brussels. They wouldn't get to see Leif as much. They moved all the way to New York just to be near us."

"Yes, and they helped you go to Columbia and do your PhD, so you'd get a plum position working in international relations. They'll be happy and proud of you."

"They'll think I should put motherhood and marriage first," I replied.

"Why first?" Candace said, sounding defiant. "Why do women have to be the ones to always put the career on the back burner while they have kids and a husband? Why not the husband?"

I sighed. "Luke has all the money," I said, feeling bad that I said it, but it was true. His money would allow us to pursue both our passions. But we both might have to compromise to ensure it happened.

"I can always wait for another opportunity at the UN in New York," I added. "That way, Luke could stay here where he had the Astra Investment headquarters. He could fly to other locations for any launches that took place, but that was in the future — not near term."

"Luke could also always fly to the USA for any launches that, as you say, aren't going to happen for a while. He's still in the investment phase and nowhere near even designing a rocket, am I right?"

Of course, she was right. We'd talked enough about Luke's plans and what stage the company was in.

"You're right. But I don't want a conflict between us over our careers. We're both ambitious, and we both want to work in our fields. Problem is, which one of us is going to compromise so that we can both be happy?"

"Why compromise? Each of you can do what you want, but it will mean travel. Either you give up this job offer and stay in New York, hope for something at the UN, or you all move to Brussels, and Luke flies back and forth between Belgium and the US. I think the answer is clear."

I exhaled in frustration. It seemed clear to Candace, but to me, it was a terrible dilemma.

Luke was so close to getting a consortium of funders and experts together that could tackle the job of setting up a space-faring company to mine the asteroid belt. Yes, it was a big dream and ambitious, given the level of technology we had, but that would just mean hiring the right people and making sure they had enough money to see it through.

Luke had the money. He had the drive and ambition.

He just had to find the right funders and experts.

I didn't want my desires to conflict with his.

How could they not conflict?

"I'll see what he says when he gets home tonight. Maybe he'll have some solution."

Candace made a sound of disapproval. "I don't want to see you compromise, kiddo. Stick to your guns. This is a dream opportunity for you. Free childcare on site? Flexible hours? The chance to work on a big project in international relations? You have to want it. You have to take it. Luke will just have to agree."

"Like I said, I'll see what he says. Until then, I'll keep my options open."

"How long do you have to respond to her offer?"

"Next week, Monday at the latest."

"I can see you're going to have a very intense weekend. If you need a shoulder to cry on or a girl's night out, I'm there for you."

"Thanks," I said. "I'll probably need it. Maybe brunch on Sunday? At our old haunt?"

"That sounds just like what the doctor ordered."

I smiled to myself and said goodbye.

Then, I sat staring out the window at the beach below the property. It would be hard to leave our beach house. I loved it and enjoyed taking Leif on a daily walk along the beach. I loved to sail and of course, my parents had recently moved nearby so they could be part of Leif's life.

Could I give all this up for the position in Brussels?

It was a dream opportunity, like Candace said.

Still, I had the dream life when it came right down to it.

Handsome wealthy husband who loved and supported my dreams. Healthy baby. Almost finished my PhD. Family nearby to take over when Luke and I needed a night off.

I waited, a sense of nervous anxiety in my gut, for Luke to return home...

CHAPTER 11

Luke

THE FOUR OF US MET AT THE RESTAURANT DOWN THE street from the Astra offices, and when we arrived, the place was packed with diners. Elena and Jack were already there and had a prime booth for us along the wall by the rear windows looking out over the patio.

"Hello," Jack said when we arrived at the table. He stood and extended his hand for a shake. We shook all around and then sat down. Immediately, a cocktail waitress came by and took our drink orders. I asked for a non-alcoholic beverage while everyone else had something stronger. I wanted to be able to help Alexa when I got home in case she'd had a hard day and wanted me to take Leif.

"You're not having a drink?" Elena asked, pointing to my bottle of seltzer when it came.

"No, I have to be a good papa when I go home," I said. "No drinking until Leif is in bed for the night."

S. E. LUND

She pouted and glanced at Jack. "Glad I'm not a parent," she said and then picked up her glass of wine, holding it up. "To all the single girls."

"To the single girls," Jack said and held up his martini. John laughed and held up his beer. A glance passed between Jack and Elena that looked surprisingly like it was meaningful in a way that suggested they were lovers rather than just business partners.

If so, it didn't surprised me. It was common for people to get together when they worked together closely. It was something I'd seen quite a lot — secretaries sleeping with their bosses, and other combinations. I didn't plan on partaking in anything like that, but it didn't surprise me that Jack might be sleeping with Elena.

It wouldn't be the first time and it wouldn't be the last that co-workers slept together.

I took a sip of my seltzer and turned to Jack.

"Elena said there were some exciting developments you wanted to fill us in on?"

Jack smiled and took another sip of his martini, then swirled the olive around before popping it in his mouth.

"I do, in fact. We just got another buy-in on the deal, so we're able to offer another fifty percent over what we originally came with. That should help in development for the next few years."

I glanced at John, who was as surprised as I was. Another fifty percent on top of what was already on offer was amazing. We could really do something with that. It would mean we would have almost double what we initially targeted for the start-up funding we would be searching for.

"That's great," I said and held up my bottle of seltzer. "Who is the new investment partner?"

"That's still under wraps, but rest assured that they are

a big *big* player in the aerospace industry and are really excited about partnering with us."

"Great!" John said and smiled. He turned to me and smiled. "Don't you think it's great?"

I smiled back. "I'd like to know who this mystery investor is."

"You'll find out soon enough. Rest assured you'll be happy. He's one of the biggest investors in the industry. His only catch is that the head office be relocated to Austin, Texas. It's a tax-free state and is really trying to promote business, so it's totally business friendly."

I made a face. "We can have a subsidiary office there, but head office? I don't think so. My home is New York."

"Come on, Luke," John said. "Texas would be great. Think about the weather. Houston is a great city. Besides, Campbell wants us to move operations there, too."

I shrugged and took a sip of my seltzer. I didn't like the idea at all. Not when John mentioned that Campbell wanted it. Not now that some other big investor wanted it.

Texas was a wasteland as far as jobs for Alexa. She wasn't ready yet to start working but hoped to soon. All she had to do was finish her PhD and then I knew she'd either get a job at a university teaching international relations, or work with some Non-Governmental Organization or with the UN or some other international body.

"We'll consider," I said, not willing to commit to anything yet. "I'd like to know more about the investor. That's important."

"He has a great reputation. I'm sure you'll be pleased."

"Why can't we know now?" I turned to Jack. "What is he waiting for?"

Jack waved his hand in dismissal. "Just getting the i's dotted and the t's crossed on the financing before making the offer so there's no doubt. Plus, he doesn't want any bad publicity in case the deal doesn't go through."

"Okay," I said hesitantly. "I'll wait to see the offer and the name of this mystery investor, and we'll decide at that point. As to Houston? I can always commute, I guess. I don't think Alexa will be interested in moving to Texas. Not with her career interests."

"Surely she can compromise," Elena said, sitting up straighter like she was somehow indignant at the thought I'd consider Alexa's interest in the matter. "This is a multi-billion-dollar deal. That must count a lot in your decision making."

"We'll wait and see the offer," I said, unwilling to budge. In other words, I had to approve the money and the man before I'd approve the deal. Sure, there was a considerable aerospace industry in Houston because of the NASA launches in the past, but so was there in Florida, and California was also an option. Plus, there was the European Space Agency located in Paris...

"It's exciting," John said, and I could see he was really happy with the potential joint venture with Jack's mystery investor. He might have been excited, but I was having misgivings. Sure, I wanted the money — it would make a huge difference to the business.

But who was the investor? Why Texas?

That was the issue for me.

For the rest of the lunch, I was pretty quiet, listening to John and Jack and Elena discussing the potential move to Houston and the future of Astra. I felt like they were viewing it as a done deal before we even knew who our new partner was.

"You're pretty quiet," John said after we said goodbye

when our lunch was finished. He walked me out to the parking lot.

"I don't understand the secrecy. Why not express a public interest in the venture? As they say, no publicity is bad publicity."

"I don't know, but with that kind of investment, I think we need to humor the guy, whoever he is. Whatever the case, we'll know more after the dinner meeting with him and the rest of the board on Saturday."

"Of course," I said.

We got into the limo, and I gave the driver instructions to take us back to the offices. John wanted to be dropped off and I wanted to go home.

On the way, I checked my cell to see if there were any messages from Alexa.

LUKE: How is Leif? Is he feeling better?

I waited and, in a moment, she texted back.

ALEXA: He's still stuffed up but is fine otherwise. Fever is down. He's feeding well.

LUKE: Good. I'll be home soon. Want me to pick something up on the way?

ALEXA: No, I have things in hand. Chicken and salad, okay?

LUKE: More than okay. By the way, we have a new mystery business partner attending the dinner meeting in Manhattan.

ALEXA: Exciting. Any hints about who?

LUKE: Nope. Everyone's lips are zipped.

ALEXA: Must be a really big shot if so.

LUKE: Hope so. See you soon. XO

ALEXA: OX

After I dropped John off at the office, I sat back and tried to relax on my way back to the beach house, glad that we would get to meet our mystery investor that weekend. Hopefully, if we spent some time with him, we'd get a better sense of what his ideas and vision was for the joint venture.

It was when we were about halfway there that I got a strange email from a name I didn't recognize. It didn't go to my spam folder, so it must have come from a legitimate email sender.

I opened it and read the contents.

Dear Mr. Marshall:

You might want to talk to your local police and ask them to investigate the garage in Westhampton that serviced your father's company car, in particular the vehicle maintenance records from the month before the crash.

If you have any questions, you can contact me at the number below my signature.

Sincerely,

Brian George, PI

What the...

What was he suggesting? That there was something nefarious about the crash that the vehicle maintenance records would reveal?

I called the number, and it went directly to voice mail.

Hello, you have reached the voice mail of Brian George, Private Investigator with George Investigations, LLC. Please leave a detailed message at the tone and I'll get back to you ASAP.

I wasn't sure what to do, or whether the guy was legit, so I decided to leave a message.

Hello, this is Luke Marshall, returning your call. Please call me with some details. Thanks.

I ended the call and sat in silence, wondering what the hell was going on...

He was obviously suggesting that there was a maintenance issue — sabotage? — that led to the car accident that killed my parents.

Then, I sat back in the vehicle and watched the roads as we made our way back to the beach house.

What the hell was going on?

Just as we were driving up to the road that bordered the beach and led to our house, Brian George called me back.

"Hello, Mr. Marshall? This is Brian George. I'm sorry to be the bearer of bad news, but I've been on a case that has turned up some interesting info on the deaths of your parents. I was wondering if we could meet and discuss."

"What was the case?"

"It's a completely different case, the details of which I'm not permitted by law to reveal, but suffice to say that in my investigation, I interviewed an inmate at the prison in New Jersey, and he had some interesting things to say about a job he had around the time your father and mother were killed in the accident. He said, and I quote, 'Usually, we fix brakes and brake lines. For this job, we did the opposite. It paid well, so who was I to question?' You should know that this man has a very long criminal record and has been diagnosed with terminal cancer. I guess this is his chance to come clean."

I frowned and felt my heart speed up. "Can you hold for a moment? I'm just driving up to my house. I'll call you back and we can talk undisturbed."

"Sure thing. I'll be waiting."

The limo drove up to the beach house to drop me off. I grabbed my briefcase and went inside. Alexa was waiting for me, baby Leif in her arms. She smiled when she saw me, and we made eye contact.

"There Mr. Big Daddy is," she said to Leif and held him up so I could give his forehead a kiss. Seeing them made some of the darkness that descended over me lift just a bit.

"It's so good to see you both, but I have a call I have to take. I'll be back in a few minutes."

"Okay. Then we can sit on the patio while the chicken roasts."

"Sounds good."

I shucked off my shoes and jacket and then went directly to my office, where I took out my laptop and opened it up. I did a quick google search on Brian George and George Investigations LLC. He was legit and was a former NYPD detective who had retired after an injury, so he was trustworthy.

I called his number.

We spoke and for the next ten minutes, he told me about the perp he had been interviewing and what the guy had to say. From what Brian could see, the perp was hoping to clear his conscience and was confessing to old crimes he'd been involved in but never charged.

At the time my parents had been killed in the accident, the man was working at a garage and had been legitimately trying to make a living as an apprentice mechanic. He'd been asked to do a very special job, and that involved 'fixing' a brake line. Brian played a recording for me.

A man's voice, a bit gruff and definitely with a Jersey twang, spoke.

"I asked him about what would happen, and he said that he'd got a job for us and if I complied, I'd get a nice fat wad of money and that was all I needed to know. It would never be traceable to me. I protested that someone could get hurt, and he assured me that it was just payback for someone who failed to do their due diligence, and no one would get hurt. Then, I read about the crash and the death of the two rich

people, and I realized it was the limo I'd worked on. I realized I was involved even if only tangentially and had no knowledge of what would happen or who was targeted."

Brian ended the recording and I sighed. "Were you able to find out who was paying him to do the job?"

"That's what we're working on right now, but given what I learned, I'm going to police but I thought you'd like to know first."

"Thanks," I said. "I appreciate the head's-up. We never thought it was anything but an accident. The police ruled it an accident, brake failure leading to loss of control on wet roads. I was assured everyone involved did their jobs and had come to the right conclusion."

"Well, hopefully, we'll find out who's behind it when the new cold case team gets hold of the details and interviews the suspect."

We spoke for a few more moments about what would happen next, and then said goodbye, with Brian's assurance that he would keep me updated, and that police would probably be contacting me for more information depending on how the investigation went.

"Be patient," Brian said. "These things take time, but we've got some good intel and so I hope police will be able to reopen the case and do some more investigation. Find out who is behind this."

"Thanks," I said and then ended the call.

I sat for a moment, not knowing what to think or do. Alexa popped her head in and gave me a smile.

"What's up? You ready for a drink?"

I rubbed my face and nodded. "Sorry. I had a very interesting phone call from a Private Investigator."

"Oh?" she said and walked beside me down the stairs. "What about?"

"You aren't going to believe it."

I could barely believe it myself.

My parents hadn't died in a tragic accident on the highway.

They'd been murdered.

CHAPTER 12

Alexa

"WHAT?"

I handed Luke a cold beer. We went to the patio to sit while supper was cooking. I put Leif in his playpen, and he was happy to sit and play with some toys laid around him.

"Apparently, the mechanic is trying to clear his conscience because of a terminal cancer diagnosis and told the investigator some info about an old job he'd worked. It sounds like someone paid him serious money to damage the brake line in a company-owned vehicle. That company appears to be my father's company. It was the week before the crash."

"Oh, Luke," I said and leaned over to give him a kiss. "I'm so sorry. That's horrible news. Who do you think might have wanted your parents killed?"

Beside me, Luke took a long pull at his beer. "Who

benefitted the most from their deaths? None other than the Marshalls."

"Oh, my God..." I glanced out over the ocean, trying to imagine Mr. Marshall arranging to have the company limo sabotaged so that Luke's parents would die in a crash. "I can't believe it. It can't be your stepfather..."

"Doesn't have to be him," Luke said. "Could have been her. Of the two of them, she's the one I'd suspect."

"Do you really think she'd be capable of plotting to have someone killed?"

Luke shrugged. "Like I said, of the two of them..." He glanced at me. "Remember what she did to you. Not something your average mother-in-law does to a daughter-in-law."

I sat for a moment in complete shock, imagining the two Marshalls, acting together or one of them on their own, to set up Luke's parents — Mr. Marshall's business partner and supposed best friend. But how many cases had I read about over the years or seen on one of those cold case or detective shows about business partners killing the other for the sake of money?

Too many.

"What about the police? Why didn't this jailhouse snitch tell police? Why was a PI contacting you?"

Luke shook his head and glanced at me. "I have no idea. The snitch has no evidence and so the police aren't investigating. He contacted a PI to get someone interested."

I sighed and considered it. If the Marshall's — one or the other — or both — arranged to damage the brakes in the company car, I would expect the local police to investigate, even if it was twenty years later.

"Why wouldn't the police investigate at least — check out the story?"

"Maybe they did and found nothing or not enough to do anything about it. It might be one of those he-said she-said kind of thing."

"But surely there would be some evidence. Did the guy actually work for the auto shop that did the maintenance on the company car? Was he an associate with the bad guy? Did the mechanic get a payoff to his bank account? That kind of thing."

Luke smiled sadly. "You sound like an amateur sleuth."

I took a sip of my non-alcoholic beer. "What does the PI think? What did you say his name was?"

"Brian George. I checked out his company. It's legit and he's a former detective in the Major Crimes Unit. Used to investigate fraud and missing persons. He thinks there's something to it and that's good enough for me. I think I'm going to have to hire him to do more sleuthing."

"Do you think that's why he contacted you? To solicit business? Is it wise to use him? Maybe find someone else."

Luke made a doubtful face. "He knows police work. He knows the system. I'll see what he charges and see what I can find out."

I sighed heavily and pondered what it all meant. If someone paid to have the brakes damaged, they must have benefitted from the death of Luke's parents in some way. If not the Marshalls, who?

"You should look back at the company's history. See if there were any grudges from former employees or executives. Would anyone have a grudge against your parents — other than the Marshalls, who were supposedly best friends. On the off chance, it was someone other than them, I mean..."

Luke leaned over and gave me a kiss. "You have such an

analytical mind... You'd be a good cop. You should consider a career in law enforcement..."

I laughed when I saw his grin and knew he was joking. I shook my head. "No thanks. Speaking of careers, guess who called me today?" When I saw a blank look on Luke's face, I realized there would be no way he could guess.

"It was an old advisor for my MA. She wants me to join her in Brussels, Belgium as an analyst."

"What?" Luke sat up and met my eyes. "She offered you a job?"

I bit my bottom lip. "I know this is really inconvenient for you, given the upcoming deal, so I wanted to talk to you about logistics before I got back to her with a definite no."

Luke glanced away and stared out over the ocean. In the distance, clouds were forming on the horizon, and it looked like a storm was brewing.

"I know it would be really difficult to have me working in Brussels, but it would only be for one year and would be great experience to use to build my resume. I'd have to be there, with Leif, but you could fly back and forth between Brussels and New York. It's not a really great flight, with one stop and it's eleven hours with the layover in Paris, but if you needed to attend a meeting, you could fly to New York, stay for the meeting and do some business, and then fly back. You could do FaceTime or Zoom the rest of the time if you needed to conduct meetings..."

Luke glanced at me. "You really like the idea."

"I do, but I understand if you think it's impossible. I know Astra has a lot going on right now, with the deal coming up and everything. I know you want to get started moving forward on the agenda, but this is what I've always wanted..."

"I want you." Luke took my hand and smiled, but I

could see his smile was sad, like he was torn about the job. "I want you happy."

Hell, I was torn about it. I had a new baby. I had really just started to feel at home at the beach house. I wasn't even finished my dissertation yet...

"I want you," I said. "I want you happy, too. What do you think? Tell me the truth..."

He sighed. "Well, to tell you the truth, this deal is an issue. The new investor and the new mystery partner want to move the headquarters to Texas."

"Texas?" I said, unable to keep the tone out of my voice. It wasn't that I had anything against Texas per se, but it was so far away from everything in my world. My parents, my school, and most of all, any job prospects in my chosen field. 'That's quite far away."

"I know," Luke said and kissed my hand. "I told the partner that I wasn't really planning on moving the head offices anywhere. I could see having a regional office there, since there is a whole culture and commercial region built up around aerospace in Texas, but not the head offices. He was all about the tax situation and said he didn't like the state taxes on corporations and individuals in New York."

"They don't pay corporate or personal tax in Texas?"

Luke nodded. "Apparently not. The new partners like that and want to move the project head offices there. There are other taxes in Texas, but the situation is beneficial to a corporation like Astra and whatever partnership we create.

I didn't say anything, not able to imagine moving to Texas. It would be a desert for my career.

"I suppose it could be me who commuted from Texas to New York or Brussels. You could stay in Texas while I flew around the world, but my job would require me to be in Brussels during the week. I wouldn't want to be away from

Leif, and there would be childcare on site so I could see him any time during the day that I had free..."

"It sounds like a great opportunity for you," Luke said. "Working for who?"

I described my former advisor and the work she was doing for an NGO located in Brussels. I talked about the job responsibilities, and the benefits and pay, including the childcare on site, which I really liked.

But I really didn't like the idea of being separated from Luke during the week or the idea that he or I would have to fly eleven hours at a minimum to get to and from our locations.

It seemed unworkable.

I sighed, and to be honest, tears sprung to my eyes. I had initially thought it would be fine for Luke to be with me in Brussels and fly to New York when he needed. He found that a trip into Manhattan once or twice every two weeks for the day was more than enough and he did meetings on Zoom. The rest of the work he could do from his own office in the beach house.

"Hey," Luke said and squeezed my hand. "Don't worry about it. We'll work something out if this is what you really want." He leaned over and kissed me on the cheek.

I wiped my eyes and forced a smile, but I really didn't know what to do or what to think about the job. It was only for a year but would be a great addition to my CV and would look good if something even better came up, like with the UN in New York, which is what I really wanted.

I didn't want to leave New York, although I had often considered moving to some other European country for international relations work. But that was before Luke and Leif...

"I have to give her a reply by Monday."

"We can talk about it this weekend. I can try to talk to the new investors and see about opening a regional office in Houston that they can staff and run and keep the head office in New York. There's always a workaround. Nothing is written in stone."

I sighed and watched Leif playing with his toys in his playpen. He was plump and happy and was benefitting from both Luke's and my attention for the past few months. To be honest, the job offer was premature. I didn't plan on working until Leif was a year old and I was finished my dissertation. I figured I'd get some entry-level job in international relations after that year was up, hopefully in New York and would work my way up. I might be able to do a Post-Doc somewhere in Europe, in England or France and make connections in the academic world. Teaching at a university was always an option if I wanted it.

It was at that point that I made my decision.

I was going to turn down the job offer — neither Leif nor I were ready for it. I wanted more months at home with him before I put him in daycare. Even if the daycare was located on site in Brussels, it would mean he was being cared for by someone other than me for most of the day. I would have weekends and holidays and that was it.

That would come soon enough, but I wanted it to be when Leif was ready for it. When he was at least a year old. I was thinking eighteen months, to be honest.

There were a lot of mothers who had to leave their babies and work soon after delivery. Why have all the money Luke had and not be able to take advantage of time home with your child?

"I'm going to say no," I said out loud, staring at the ocean down below the beach house property.

Luke squeezed my hand. "Don't say no yet. Let it percolate over the weekend. You have until Monday..."

I shook my head. "No. It's too soon. I planned on staying home with Leif for at least a year — eighteen months if possible. This job offer sounds great in principle, but it's just not right for us at this time." I turned to Luke and met his eyes. "That's the reality of it. It's not good for me or Leif or us. I'll tell her on Monday, but the answer will be no."

Luke kissed my hand. "It's your decision."

"No, it's our decision. It's all three of our lives. I have to think of all of us when I decide."

Luke didn't say anything, but his expression told me he was relieved that I would be saying no.

He had enough issues to deal with considering the new investors wanting to move to Texas and the fact that his adoptive parents might have arranged his parents' deaths.

I didn't want a job in Belgium to be another.

CHAPTER 13

Luke

"What do you think?" Alexa stood in front of the mirror on the closet wall and turned sideways, staring at her reflection.

She didn't look happy.

"You look wonderful."

She shook her head. "This is still too tight around the belly," she said and unzipped the side zipper. It was my favorite black dress, one that showed off her ample curves, and I loved it.

She was right — it was still a bit tight around the belly, but that was to be expected since it had been only just over six months since Leif was born.

It was going to take Alexa a while to get back into fighting form. I didn't care — she was just as desirable to me now as she had been before Leif was born, but I knew Alexa was critical of her efforts to regain her pre-baby figure, despite my protests to the contrary.

She spent some time standing in front of her wardrobe, looking at one dress after the other, pulling them out and then considering them, one hand over her mouth.

"This one will have to do," she said and pulled out one of her maternity dresses that had a gather below the bodice allowing for the swell of a pregnant belly. "Will you be embarrassed to attend this dinner with your new investor with me in this dress?" she asked, her brow furrowed. "I mean, it's a maternity dress..."

"Didn't I tell you how beautiful you looked in that dress?" I went to her and pulled her into my arms, kissing her passionately.

"Yes, you did, but that was because I was pregnant."

"You looked beautiful because you are beautiful. You were beautiful pregnant and you're beautiful now, no longer pregnant."

"And still have a belly with too much fat," she said and pulled out of my arms, holding the dress up in front of her. "Does it make me look a bit pasty? It is pretty pale..."

"You could never look pasty," I said and stood behind her, my arms slipping around her waist. "You look tasty," I said, smiling to myself. "Like dessert. Which I intend to indulge tonight after dinner."

"You do, do you?" Alexa replied, her eyes meeting mine in the mirror.

"I do," I said and turned her around, kissing her once more, one hand roving down her back to the soft swell of her breast. "I intend to get my fill of you."

"You can fill me any time," she replied, a leer in her eye. I kissed her again, my own body responding to the feel of her breasts pressed against my chest.

"That's a date," I said, and she slipped out of my arms and removed the dress from its hanger and slipped it over her head. She adjusted it and turned from side to side, eyeing herself in it.

"Do I look okay? Presentable?"

"You look delicious," I said and ran my hands down her arms.

"Well, this will have to do."

She went to the bathroom to finish her hair while I slipped on a clean white shirt and fastened my tie. When we were both ready, we went downstairs and Alexa wrote down a list of instructions for her parents, who had arrived about half an hour earlier, just in time to put Leif went down for his afternoon nap.

After talking about Leif's evening's feed and the expressed breastmilk in the fridge and going over the details of the dinner meeting we were having with the new investor, we went to the front entrance to leave.

"You look lovely, dear," Alexa's mom said and gave her a quick hug. "Both of you."

"Thanks, Mom," I said and kissed her.

Alexa's dad smiled. "You do. You guys look like a few billion bucks."

Alexa laughed at that and kissed her father.

Then, the two of us left, taking the steps down to the waiting limo.

WE ARRIVED at the venue and went inside. The restaurant was a steakhouse in the financial district, where a lot of high rollers on Wall Street went for meals and drinks. I suspected that our investor, who still remained anonymous up until that night, was a player on Wall Street and that was why he wanted to stay quiet about the possible investment. He didn't want to affect the value of his own company's stock or Astra's eventual IPO. Astra was still a private corporation and hadn't gone public yet, so we didn't have stock trading on any exchange, but one day, we would.

We entered the glittering glass and gilded interior and were immediately struck by the candlelight, the soft music and the dozens of tables with white linen tablecloths, lots of crystal and silverware. It was definitely high-end.

Most of all, we were shocked to find the place was empty.

There were no other patrons.

In the rear of the room next to a brick wall with windows overlooking the street was one large table, and that was where our mystery investor sat, with John and Felicia, Jack Tate and his wife, Adam Pierce and a woman I didn't know but assumed was his wife, Elena Marakova. Beside them sat Frank Campbell and a woman I assumed was his wife.

Beside them, the man himself.

Ken Hanson.

The Ken Hanson of Hanson Investments Inc., one of the largest hedge funds on Wall Street.

The Ken Hanson of Northwestern Airlines, of Hanson Industries, which created tech for the military, and the Ken Hanson who was partnered with one of the biggest aerospace companies that worked with NASA.

We stood at the hostess station and waited for the hostess to escort us. She was on the phone and held a finger up to stop us.

"It's Ken Hanson," Alexa whispered, while we waited

for the hostess to finish her call. "No wonder they wanted to keep it secret."

I squeezed her around the waist, my heart rate increasing at the prospect that Hanson wanted to invest in Astra's joint venture.

That was incredible news.

It was beyond my expectations. I could have written down five big investors whom I would want to partner with, and his name was definitely on the list. Hell, it was at the very top.

"I can't believe it's him. He's the mystery investor."

"I know."

"Sorry for the wait," the hostess said. "You're Luke Marshall?"

"Yes," I replied. "We're meeting that party." I gestured to the table. John glanced over and saw me. He stood and waved.

He must have been just as excited as I was.

"Right this way," the hostess said and led us through the restaurant to the table in the back of the room.

We arrived at the table and Adam Pierce and Jack Tate both stood up, Adam pulling out a chair for Alexa and Jack extending a hand to shake.

"Hello," Jack said. "Glad you could make it. Luke Marshall, may I introduce Frank Campbell and his wife Donna, and Ken Hanson, who you might know as the CEO of Hanson Investments and other interests. Ken, this is the man of the hour. Luke Marshall of Astra Investments."

Frank and Ken stood and extended their hands, and I shook Frank's first, since he was closer. Then, I turned to Ken and was struck by how piercing his ice blue eyes were, his dark hair shot through with streaks of silver, his jaw square. He was former military and looked it with a near-brush cut. His suit was impeccable, and his grip firm.

"Ken, really pleased to meet you."

"The same," Ken said, and he turned to Alexa. "You must be Mrs. Alexandria Marshall. We've heard so much about you from John. International relations PhD, right?"

Alexa shook Ken's hand and smiled. "Nice to meet you as well."

We all sat finally, and the cocktail waitress arrived to take our drink orders. I ordered a craft beer and Alexa ordered her usual virgin Pina Colada.

"Oh, you drink those?" Elena said, sounding surprised. "I love them, but they have so many calories. It must be quite hard to lose the baby weight. I can't imagine. Denying yourself all the food you ate before you gave birth."

Elena smiled and took a sip of her glass of white wine.

The dig wasn't lost on me. I reached over and squeezed Alexa's hand, which was on the bench seat beside me.

"Actually, it's not hard at all. I'm busy with Leif and happy with how things are going. I'm lucky."

Alexa smiled brightly. If the dig hurt her, she wasn't going to let Elena know it.

"You look beautiful as always, Alexa," Felicia said, her voice soft as usual. She actually blushed when speaking. "How lucky you are to have it all."

"I am lucky," Alexa said and squeezed my hand.

"We're all lucky," Elena said. "Lucky to see such talented players in the aerospace industry brought together to invest in the future."

I turned to Ken, and he turned to me, expectantly. "I'm really pleased to know that you're the mystery investor who wants to partner with us."

"I couldn't wait for us to meet," he said with a guilty

smile. "Sorry to keep this under wraps, but we didn't want people to think we were doing a pump and dump as a way to increase the value of our company, or yours. Better to wait until the deal is signed, sealed and delivered."

"I agree," I said and held up my bottle of beer. "Don't want the FEC breathing down our necks."

"At least not any more than they already do, right?"

"Right," I said and took a sip, pleased that he was so interested in Astra. He was no small player but was instead one of the biggest and most notorious aerospace investors in the business. I never for a moment imagined that the new investor was him or his company.

"To the future," Ken said and stood, his glass raised. "To bringing the very best minds in the aerospace industry together to solve tomorrow's problems and bring even more value to our shareholders."

"Hear, hear," I replied and raised my bottle. We all toasted each other and took a drink then Ken sat back down. For the next hour, he peppered me with questions about my history, although he revealed enough details to show he'd done his homework — or at least, had read the précis on me and Astra provided to him by his assistants. He had a sharp mind and was anything if not forward-thinking and future oriented.

I was more than excited to have Ken on board. In fact, I figured that if we could seal the deal, it would mean Astra would be a real serious player in the industry.

The sky was the limit, in other words.

I took Alexa's hand under the table and squeezed it, then turned to look in her eyes. I could see she was happy with the way the evening had gone so far.

I couldn't wait to get home with her alone...

CHAPTER 14

Alexa

I squeezed Luke's hand and smiled at how eager he looked at the fact that Ken was the mysterious investor who wanted to buy a stake in Astra. Adam Pierce and Elena Marakova of Seneca were important, as was Jack Tate, but Ken Hanson...

He was the real deal. Even bigger than Frank Campbell.

During the evening, I felt the men's eyes on me, appraising me as Luke's partner. I knew I would get the once-over by them and hoped I didn't disappoint.

But it was the gaze of Elena that felt the most uncomfortable.

When we were nearly finished dinner, I had to excuse myself and went to the washroom for a pee break. I left the table and made my way to the rear of the restaurant, and then went into a stall.

I was just washing my hands and adjusting my hair when Elena walked in.

"Isn't it so like us girls to do bathroom break together?" she said as she stood beside me and adjusted her own hair.

I smiled but didn't respond. I wasn't a girl and didn't ask for her to accompany me.

"That's a nice very conservative dress," she said and adjusted her bodice, which revealed her ample breasts. She gave me a once over. "I guess that now that you're a mother, the dresses you used to wear are off-limits, am I right? Are you back to your pre-pregnancy weight yet?" She stood back and tilted her head, looking at my midsection. "Are you breastfeeding?" She leaned forward and put her hand on my arm. "My sister said her breasts were never the same afterward. Plus, she said she had zero libido. They divorced soon after and he found a younger woman. It can't be good for a healthy marriage."

I didn't know what to say in response. Each one of her comments was a clear barb directed at me and my desirability, now that I was a mother and had given birth and was breastfeeding.

"Excuse me," I said and brushed by her, not wanting to say what I really thought so I didn't cause any problems with the deal. "I need to get back." I gave her a smile and left the washroom.

I arrived back at the table and the men were courteous enough to stand when I arrived, and Luke held out my chair. I sat and smiled and then picked up my virgin Pina Colada and took a big sip, wishing it was the real deal instead of virgin. I needed it after my brief encounter with Elena Marakova.

Soon enough, she arrived back, and the men likewise stood for her.

I had to admit she looked like a million bucks. Her dress was very expensive and sexy, showing off her obviously inflated breasts and her lipstick accentuating her filled lips.

She smiled at me, raising her shoulder just a bit like she was coy.

She was a hateful bitch.

I saw right through her, familiar with her type in high school. I didn't let them get to me back then, and I certainly wasn't going to let one get to me now.

She was clearly jealous. Why else be so mean? I didn't think she was just unaware of how she had put me down so many times in the washroom.

She had to know.

Did she have a thing for Luke? Or did she just resent any happy marriage where the woman had a baby and was a stay-at-home mom?

"So, what's on the agenda for you, Alexa?" Ken asked. "What are your plans now that you've just had a baby? I hear you're doing your PhD in International Relations at Columbia."

I turned to him and smiled. "I'm going to finish my dissertation once things settle down with Leif and I get into the swing of things. Once I'm finished and have defended my dissertation, I could get a post-doc and work somewhere, teaching or I could work in the NGO field. Maybe work for a politician as an advisor. That kind of thing."

"Will you want to stay in New York, or will you want to move somewhere else?" Felicia asked.

"I'd think she'll have to locate wherever Astra is located, considering Luke's position as CEO and Chairman of the Board," Elena said. She gave me a quick smile. "Isn't that right?"

"The future is open for Alexa," Luke said and put his

arm around my shoulders. "Once she's ready, I'm sure she'll get a position she wants in the field. If that's New York and she's at the UN, that works out fine. If she's in Paris or Brussels, so be it. Luckily, we're pretty flexible and can travel and I can still run Astra from wherever we live."

"Speaking of which, there are a few details that have to be worked out," Ken said. "I think once they are, we will be able to go ahead and put the merger in place."

"Merger?" Luke said, and we could all hear the surprise in Luke's voice that Ken used that term. "You mean joint venture, right? Astra and Seneca will remain privately owned, as I'm sure Campbell will. We'll simply be offering Hanson a share position in the consortium with seats on the board. I thought that was understood." Luke turned to John, frowning. "That was the offer, right?"

John turned to Frank, Elena and Adam, who leaned forward.

"That was my understanding. Ken," Adam said. "Why don't you tell us why you think there was going to be a merger?"

"I thought it was understood. I want Astra and Seneca to come under the Hanson umbrella as two of our subsidiaries. Luke and Adam will remain CEOs, but Astra and Seneca will be part of the Hanson empire. I think having one large corporation at the helm will be so much better for this project than a consortium, Too much red tape. Too many competing interests."

Luke shook his head. "That wasn't my understanding. I wouldn't have agreed to this if it had been. I want Astra to remain my company. John's and my company. We want investors who will partner with us, not buy us out. I'm sure Adam feels the same."

Adam shrugged and held his hands up. "I'm not quite

sure what to say. This is a surprise." He turned to Elena, who tilted her head to the side, acting all innocent.

"I can assure you that it's a very sweet deal," Ken replied.

"I'm not doing this for the money," Luke said.

Ken leaned back and glanced around the table. "There seems to have been some kind of misunderstanding. I think we'll need to do some more work on this before we can talk further. My apologies if this wasn't communicated properly."

With that, Ken stood up, placed his napkin on his plate, and nodded in Luke's direction and then Adam's. "Luke, Adam, I'll have my people call your people. We'll meet again, hopefully once it's all cleared up."

He nodded to me and the rest of the group and then left, heading out the door without looking back.

"Well, that was a big fucking waste of time," Adam Pierce said. "I want to know who's responsible for this fuck up." He stood and pulled out Elena's chair, who also stood. "Let's go. Luke, I'll be talking to you tomorrow."

Both Elena and Adam left the restaurant, leaving me with Jack Tate, Frank Campbell and his wife, all of whom appeared flustered.

"Did you know about this?" Luke asked Jack.

He shrugged. "It wasn't on my radar," he said. "Elena was the one who put Ken forward as a potential investor and she ran point on the matter of getting him on board. I guess we'll have to wait and see what she says."

My mouth was open, and I was still at a loss for words. "He actually thought he was buying Astra and Seneca out, and just keeping Luke and Adam on in symbolic roles? Who gave him that idea?"

"What about Campbell?" Frank asked.

Jack shook his head. "You got me. Not that it would be a bad idea to merge with Hanson. I mean, they're huge. But that wasn't what I understood the deal was about."

"Me either," Luke said.

I took his hand and squeezed, and he glanced my way, concern clear in his blue eyes.

What the hell?

Elena was a nasty bitch, and I suspected a conniving one as well.

"So, Elena never said anything about a merger when she presented the idea to you to bring Ken Hanson on board?"

Jack shook his head. "Not once."

"Wow," was all Luke could manage.

We finished our after-dinner drinks and then because of the uncomfortable silence between us, Jack stood and grabbed the bill.

"Let me get this," he said. "Rest assured I'll be speaking with Elena and Adam about this. Adam should have known about the whole merger idea and have communicated it clearly to you before tonight if that was their agenda."

"Thanks, Jack," Luke said and stood. He extended his hand. "I'm sorry that this dinner and evening seems to have been a big waste of time for you."

"No, not at all," Jack said and shook Luke's hand. "It's good to know what Ken's intentions are. He's big, but he's not the only big fish in the sea, if you're really against a merger. I'm sure if people find out that Hanson wanted to acquire Astra that Astra will be in big demand for future investments even if you say no."

"Thanks," Luke said. Beside him, John stood and shook Jack's hand as well. Frank Campbell and his wife stood, too.

We all said goodbye and watched Jack go to the bar and pay the tab, while the Campbells left the restaurant.

"Well, that was a kick in the teeth," John said after he sat back down. He put his arm around Felicia. "Talk about being blindsided."

"Exactly," Luke replied. He took my hand and kissed it then looked in my eyes. "I don't think we can trust Elena. Do you think Adam really didn't know about this? Why wouldn't Elena tell him?"

I shrugged. "I think she's a sociopath."

Luke laughed out loud at that. "I think you may be right."

"Why do you think that, Alexa?" Felicia asked, leaning forward.

"Ever since I met her, she's attacked me in these small ways that only a high school bitch would. You know the type, I'm sure. Little digs at the way you look all designed to show interest, but they're clear put-downs."

"I do know the type, sadly," Felicia said and took a sip of her wine. "Only too well. I was always the brunt of this one girl's attacks."

"What are you talking about?" John asked, his eyebrows raised. "Was Elena being rude to you?"

I sighed and considered whether to say anything. I was going to just swallow it and let things happen with her and Adam Pierce because the deal was so important to Luke, figuring that I didn't have to like Elena. What she did to me didn't matter in the long run if the deal was a good one.

"She warned me that my boobs would be ruined by breastfeeding and Luke would divorce me because I was a dried-up old woman with no sex drive, or something..."

"She said that to you?" Luke said, turning to me, an angry expression on his face.

"Not in so many words," I replied. "But that was the implication."

"What a bitch," Luke said and shook his head. "How can she think she can talk to you like that and get away with it? Not to mention misleading us about Ken's intentions. I'll have to talk to her in private."

I put my hand on Luke's arm. "I can defend myself," I said. "I don't want you thinking that you have to defend my honor or anything."

He leaned over and kissed me on the lips. "I know you can. I just want to give her a piece of my mind. You can't blame me for wanting to straighten her out."

I smiled and ran my fingers through his hair. "You're my knight in shining armor, but I have my own rapier-like wit."

"You do," he said and then turned to John. "I guess we need to go back to the drawing board if Hanson is off the menu."

"I guess," John said. "No worries. We're good. I have faith that there will soon be other better investors who want to join forces, rather than swallow us up."

"Good," Luke said. "I didn't start Astra just to sell it to the highest bidder. This is my life's work. I want to keep control."

I squeezed Luke's hand.

Astra was his life's work.

I was so proud of him that he was willing to keep control, even if it meant he would lose a huge opportunity to become ultra-rich — even richer than he was already.

We left the restaurant and said goodbye to John and Felicia. Then, we took the limo service to the apartment and after removing our evening attire, we crashed into bed. Before Luke turned off the bedside lamp, he turned to me and put his arms around me, folding me into his embrace.

"I don't know about you, Mrs. Marshall, but that was a

really shocking turn of events. I think I need some Alexa time to get over the trauma."

"Luckily, Alexa time is my expertise," I replied and kissed him.

For the next hour, we lost ourselves in each other's embrace.

Later, as I rode Luke, his hands on my breasts, and his cock filling my very needy body, I thought for a fleeting moment about Elena Marakova and her snide comments about marriage, motherhood and desire.

She could go to hell...

CHAPTER 15

Luke

WE RETURNED TO THE BEACH HOUSE ON SUNDAY, AND while Alexa's mom and dad watched Leif, Alexa and I went for a sail along the coast.

We both needed to recover from our evening with Ken Hanson, but most of all, Elena Marakova.

The salty air was good for us both, clearing our heads and energizing us.

"I feel almost ready for battle," I said to Alexa when we finished docking in our slip at the marina.

"Are you going into the city this week? I imagine there will be several meetings to clarify things."

I nodded. "I have to for a couple of days at least. But I'll come back every night. I'm not wasting my year with Leif for this."

"Good," Alexa said and helped me get the boat ready

for the next time we wanted to sail. "I can't wait until Leif is old enough to come sailing with us."

"Don't worry," I said. "We'll turn him into a good little sailor."

We drove back to the beach house and spent the afternoon with the grandparents and enjoyed watching them play with Leif. Finally, we had a nice dinner on the patio, and when the sun had set and the stars came out, Mrs. Dixon turned to me.

"This is such a beautiful home," she said. "How wonderful to be able to raise Leif here. You two are so lucky."

"We are," I replied for I knew it. I knew it with all my heart. I was going to do nothing to jeopardize that, and if it meant turning down a really sweet deal with Ken Hanson, so be it. I would love the investment dollars such a deal would afford, but I did not want to lose control of Astra. I did not want to move to Houston and commute back and forth to New York.

I was even rethinking any kind of deal with Elena Marakova.

I had a bad taste in my mouth about her willingness to just give over to Hanson. Did she not have any pride in her own company that she was happy to sell out so quickly?

As for Hanson, I understood his motivation. He wanted to buy up any promising new aerospace companies and be the biggest corporation of all providing product and services to NASA and other national space agencies.

But that wasn't my vision. It wasn't John's either.

I was sure Adam felt the same, although we hadn't had a chance to talk yet. I didn't know Campbell well enough to judge.

We said goodbye to the Dixons and after I gave Leif his

bath and handed him to Alexa for his bedtime feed, I went to the office and called John.

"Hey," I said and sat down at my desk, watching the stars rise over the ocean beyond our property. "I wanted to touch base and see what your thoughts were after our night with the gang."

"That was some night, am I right?" John replied. "What did you think about Ken Hanson being the mystery investor?" His voice sounded hesitant, like he wanted to feel me out before committing.

"I was as surprised — and pleased — as you probably were. But Houston? And a merger? That wasn't what either of us intended. Nor do I think Adam Pierce wants it."

He sighed audibly. "I know. But it's so tempting. With Hanson's money and clout, we could really do things. Fast. Much faster than without that money."

"Yeah, but a merger?" I said in protest. "If we merged with Hanson, he would have the control, and could take Astra anywhere he wanted, instead of where we want. We'd be figureheads only. Not really in control. I don't like that. Not at all."

"Geeze," John replied. "It's hard to turn that money down..."

We talked for another fifteen minutes about the coming week, unable to really conclude anything until we saw the deal in writing. As it was, it was all just verbal and speculation. We'd need some hard numbers to know for sure what we would be getting into if the deal went through.

"We'll meet tomorrow for lunch," I said and checked my watch, wanting to be able to put Leif down for the night. "We can go over what we want together and then wait for the paperwork from Hanson before we get too excited — or disappointed. In the meantime, we need to keep our options open and meet with other potential business partners."

"I agree. See you tomorrow. You want to go to Vector for lunch? I feel like a good burger."

"Sounds good. See you."

I ended the call and went back to the living room. Alexa had just finished giving Leif the breast and was burping him on her shoulder. I grabbed a receiving blanket and placed it over my shoulder and then took Leif from her so I could do the burping work. I kissed Leif's head and then placed him on my shoulder, then walked to the patio doors so he could see outside.

"What did John have to say?"

I sighed. "He was as torn as I am about it. Hanson's great, and the company has so much capital and expertise, but neither of us really want to see a merger. A joint venture, yes. A merger, no."

Alexa adjusted her nursing bra and then stood up, coming over to where Leif and I stood. A huge burp erupted from Leif's tiny mouth and so I took him off my shoulder and wiped off his mouth. He smiled at me in return, and I felt my heart surge with love.

I never knew how much love I could feel for a baby, but boy, did I know it now.

"He should be changed and go down," Alexa said, holding out her arms to take Leif.

"No, I'll do it," I said and carried Leif up the stairs to his nursery. "Make us some decaf."

"Okay."

I took Leif to his room, laid him on the change table, and then proceeded to remove his onesie, and put on a fresh diaper and clean onesie. While I did, he chewed on his hand, and generally waved his arms around, babbling back at me while I told him all about the world.

When he was all freshly changed, I placed him in his crib, gave him his pacifier, turned on the mobile over the crib, and dimmed the lights. He was absorbed by the mobile and although he waved his arms around a bit, soon he was quiet.

I closed the door after checking to see that the baby monitor light was on, indicating it was operating properly.

Then I went downstairs to Alexa.

WE SAT ON THE PORCH, cups of decaf in hand, and watched the moon transit across the sky over the ocean. It was a beautiful evening, and I felt so lucky that we had use of the house and property.

I wanted Leif to grow up here.

Not in Houston.

"What are you thinking about?" Alexa asked after a comfortable silence passed between us.

"Just how much I love it here. How much I want Leif to grow up here instead of anywhere else."

"There aren't many kids around for him to play with," Alexa said. "I've been doing some research and most of the homeowners here are either older or have turned their homes into Airbnbs for most of the year. The closest school is in quite far away. It's not really a great family neighborhood. Not like I grew up in, at least."

"You know what they say. Kids today have play dates. They don't wander. Everything is organized. Whatever school Leif goes to will have kids from the local area. We'll make it work."

Alexa turned to me and took my hand. "You really don't like the idea of moving to Houston, do you?"

"Neither do you," I replied.

"There are probably beautiful homes there in great neighborhoods. We could make it work if that was what you really wanted."

"It's not the city as much as it's the terms of the deal. I never wanted to consider a merger. Always a partnership. A joint venture where we retain control of our own businesses and just work together towards a mutual goal. That doesn't seem to be what Hanson wants."

Alexa sighed. "I know. I don't really want to move to Houston, no matter how nice it would be where we lived and how great the climate is. It's just too far away from anything for me."

"You could teach at one of the universities..."

"I could," she replied. "As a last resort. But you know me. I want to do something real. Have a real impact. Teaching at a university is great, but it's not why I'm doing my PhD. I want to get my hands dirty in the real world. That means New York, Paris, Berlin, Barcelona, Oslo, Brussels."

We sat like that for a while, hand in hand, and were silent, as each of us probably mused on why the potential deal with Hanson was not what either of us really wanted.

"I'm going to have to say no," I said finally. "There's just no way the deal is what I want. It's not my vision for Astra, and it's not my vision for our lives. Nothing against Houston or Austin, but they're both too far away for you and the merger is off the table. Officially tomorrow, but John and I will review the paperwork first and then say no."

"That's too bad," Alexa said and squeezed my hand. "I know you were really excited for the deal."

I pulled her hand up to my mouth and kissed her knuckles. "We'll find someone else to team up with. Someone with the same vision as we have. I have faith."

We sat in silence for a while, the distant sound of the surf soothing.

It was at that point that I got a call and checked the call display. Brian George. Then, I remembered the message about the maintenance of the company vehicle.

"Hey, Brian," I said when I answered. "What's up?" Beside me, Alexa sat up, her expression concerned.

"Just calling to see if we could meet this week to discuss the issue I raised earlier. When is a good time? Will you be in Manhattan, or should I come out to Westhampton?"

"I'll be in town tomorrow and can meet you then, if that's good for you."

"What time?"

"How about two? I have a lunch meeting."

"Sounds good," Brian replied. "Your office?"

"How about somewhere neutral?"

"Maybe the boardwalk near your office? That way, there would be no chance of anyone overhearing our discussions."

"You think that's necessary?"

"Oh, yeah," Brian said, his voice sounding serious. "This is not something you want to become general knowledge."

"Okay," I said. "Message me when you're in place, and I'll meet you."

We ended the call and I turned to Alexa, whose eyes were wide. "What?"

"Brian George wants to meet to discuss the issue. He thinks it would be best to meet outside so no one could spy on us."

"Seriously?"

"I guess he thinks it might be safer that way."

"You're scaring me," Alexa said. "The only people who would be spying on you would be your own parents."

"Stepparents," I replied. "While I can't believe my stepfather had anything to do with it, I do believe my stepmother could. Now that I know her better, I think she's the kind of woman who might just try to have someone killed for the insurance money and inheritance."

"It's damn scary to imagine that she did," Alexa said. "It sounds like one of those cold case shows I've watched."

"It will be hard to prove, whatever the case."

Alexa squeezed my hand and we sat in silence, both of us thinking of the implications and what it would do to my family if so.

It would literally tear us apart...

"Let's have a bath," I said and pulled Alexa into the bedroom to the master bath with the huge tub.

"I thought you'd never ask," Alexa said with a coy smile.

While I ran the bath and poured in some bubble bath, Alexa removed her clothes. I turned and saw her standing naked.

"You are so beautiful," I said, while I began removing my own clothes. Alexa helped me, smiling as she saw my rapidly growing erection.

She slipped below the water, hiding herself from me, the soap bubbles around the curve of her breasts. I sank down as well and leaned back across from her, my legs on either side of her body.

"Ahh, this is the life," I said and closed my eyes. After a moment, I opened one and met her gaze. "You're too far away. Come here. Lie on top of me."

She smiled slowly, then crawled over to me, her body floating above mine, her face just inches from mine. Her body lay between my bent knees, her arms around my shoulders.

God, she was beautiful. I breathed in deeply and licked my lips.

"Kiss me," I ordered.

She smiled, no doubt recognizing the little game I wanted to play – Dominant and submissive. She bit her bottom lip coyly, getting into character. "How would you like me to kiss you, Sir? Chastely or passionately?"

I raised one eyebrow expectantly. "You need to ask?"

I reached one hand behind her head and pulled her to me, our lips meeting in a very passionate kiss. I groaned when my tongue touched hers and pulled her even closer, reaching down to grab one deliciously rounded buttock and pulled her against my erection, which was hard and aching.

We lay like that, her body above mine, my erection pressed against her and just enjoyed the mutual desire.

"Would Sir like me to wash you?" she asked, glancing at me from below half-closed lids.

I narrowed my eyes. "Yes." I rose up on my knees in front of her, and my cock, thick and heavy, hung close to her face. "With your tongue."

She complied, taking soap in her hand and lathering up. Then, she ran her hands over my erection, cupping my balls, stroking my length.

She rinsed me off and I remained there, my cock in front of her face.

"Suck me," I ordered. She leaned forward and licked the head. I groaned with pleasure and that made her even more eager to please me. She took the head into her mouth and glanced up, making eye contact with me.

"All of it."

She did, stroking her tongue under the head before

sucking in more of my length. Then she took me even deeper before gagging. I pulled out a bit and started a smooth stroking rhythm. She took me into her mouth, then pulled off fully before taking me in once more.

"That's enough." I stood up and reached down, pulling her up. I helped her out of the tub and dried us both off. I picked her up and carried her to our bed, then lay her back.

I lay on top of her, my hard cock against her pussy, and she rubbed against it with wanton desire.

I kissed her, sucking her tongue into my mouth. I broke the kiss and began licking and kissing her all over, enjoying every inch of her skin, careful to avoid her nipples, which I kept until last just to drive her crazy.

"Oh, God," she moaned, her eyes closing.

I moved down her body, and kissed a trail down to her pussy, opening her thighs. I licked her deliberately, running my tongue all around her clit, and her opening, before slipping two fingers inside of her. She came at that, her flesh clenching around me.

"You're a needly little thing, aren't you, Lexi?"

She didn't reply, but her closed eyes and fast breathing told me everything I needed to know.

When she recovered enough, I knelt between her thighs, my shaft in my hand.

"Suck me again," I ordered.

She opened her mouth and stuck out her tongue to receive it, licking the tip. Then, she took the head in her mouth and sucked while I gripped the shaft, feeding her my cock.

I thrust slowly, enjoying the buildup of pleasure.

"I need to fuck you," I groaned when I knew I was close. I crawled lower on the bed and lifted her hips, then pressed the head against my clit, rubbing it all over her pussy. With one hand, I squeezed a breast, my thumb circling the nipple.

"You're so fucking desirable," I murmured "I want to fuck you hard."

I pressed the head of my cock against her and smiled when I heard her gasp. She needed me as much as I needed her

Then I pushed into her, filling her up, my hands gripping her hips. While I thrust, I stroked her clit, and soon, she was shuddering with her second orgasm.

"Oh God, oh God," she cried out as she came, her body clenching around my cock. That made me thrust harder, and soon, the pleasure peaked, and my ejaculation began, my own body shuddering.

"Oh, God," I groaned, thrusting deep and slow, ejaculating with each thrust.

I collapsed on top of her when I was finished, and together, we lay in each other's arms, enjoying the last throes of our mutual orgasms.

"Don't you ever let anyone make you feel less than completely beautiful and desirable," I said when we turned to face each other. I stroked her cheek. "Elena is just jealous. You're beautiful. I love you."

"I love you," she said and smiled, but I could tell there was still just a hint of doubt in her.

I planned on proving to her just how much I loved her every day of my life.

CHAPTER 16

Alexa

"What's on your agenda for today?"

Luke finished dressing while I sat in bed, Leif in my arms being fed for the first time.

"I've got to give Professor Turner an answer today," I said, admiring Luke as he pulled on a pair of slacks and fastened his belt.

"What's your answer?" He turned to me, an expectant expression on his handsome face.

He already knew what it was, but I realized he was trying to be open to yes, if I changed my mind.

"I can't say yes," I replied.

I had spent the night sleeplessly considering my decision about the job offer.

I already knew what it would be. If Luke turned down a sweetheart merger deal with Hanson because he wanted us to be somewhere nearer to where I could ultimately get a

S. E. LUND

job in my field, how could I accept this job and take Leif away from where Luke would have to spend most of his time?

Even if Luke traveled back and forth between Brussels and New York, it would be very disruptive to him, and would mean he had less time with Leif while he was growing up.

So, as much as the job appealed to me, as excited I might be about moving to Brussels and taking the job, I knew it was too soon.

Too soon to be going back to work after having Leif.

Too far away from New York.

There would be other opportunities — I was sure of it. Besides, I had to finish my PhD first.

"You can say yes," he replied finally while he slipped on a clean white shirt. He turned to face me as he did up the buttons. "We can make it work if this is what you really want. We have every resource at our disposal — a nanny if you want one, housekeepers, and I can fly back and forth."

"I know," I said. "It's just not the right time. There will be other opportunities."

He came over and leaned down, kissing me on the lips tenderly. "As long as you're happy."

"I am. Brilliantly happy."

I smiled and he kissed me again.

I finished feeding Leif and burped him, and then followed Luke to the kitchen. He quickly fixed a cup of coffee for us both while I put Leif in his seat. Luke poured himself some coffee in a travel mug and then handed me my own decaffeinated version.

"You're so thoughtful," I said.

He kissed me. "I'm so lucky."

We had a quick breakfast and then I kissed Luke

138

goodbye and held up Leif's hand to wave at Luke as he walked down the front steps to the waiting limo that would take him into the city for his day of meetings.

"Good luck with your meetings," I said, thinking about his meeting with the PI. "I'm worried about what he might tell you."

"I'll call you with any details if there's anything of note. Otherwise, we can talk when I get home. Do you want me to pick something up for dinner on my way back? Chinese? Indian? Ricardo Ribs?"

"Ooh, Ricardo Ribs, please. And lots of their coleslaw."

"Will do."

I waved goodbye. Then, I went inside and got ready for the day. When I had Leif safely in his seat, surrounded by his toys, I took out my laptop and opened it, preparing myself for my letter to Professor Turner.

I chewed a fingernail, considering my words, and then opened my mailing app and created an email to her.

Dear Professor Turner,

Thanks so much for the offer of a position with you in Brussels. As much as the offer is tempting, and as much as it would be a dream come true to work with you in the job with the NGO, I am unable, at this time, to accept. Leif is still too young to be moved halfway around the world, and I really must finish my PhD before I do anything so major. While working for you would be wonderful experience on my C.V., I feel I have to put my family first and at this time, that means I have to regretfully decline.

I wish you all the best in your endeavours and thank you once again for the offer. Please keep me in mind for the future in case you need someone and I'm available. I would love to work with you and in this field.

Yours, Alexa Dixon-Marshall

I read the email over several times, and then glanced at Leif, who had one of his toys stuffed in his mouth.

"Well, little man, this is me turning down the best job offer I've ever had."

Leif burbled around the toy in his mouth, unaware of the cruel world he would one day inherit. I sighed and sent the email off into the ether.

Then, I checked my other email and messages, and decided that instead of moping around about opportunities I couldn't accept, I would spend the morning doing research on my dissertation. That would be a better use of my time than wondering what might have been.

The morning passed quickly, and around eleven I heard my cell chime and checked my messages.

LUKE: Hey, how are you doing? You upset about having to turn down the job offer? I want you to know that you're a brilliant scholar or else Prof. Turner wouldn't have asked you to be her assistant. I'm sure you'll have numerous job offers over the years, so don't let this discourage you.

I smiled and felt my heart swell at his words.

ALEXA: I'm fine. Really. Sure, it would have been a plum job, but I want to be able to focus on Leif for his first full year. I know how lucky I am that you and I can be with him for the whole year. Many parents don't have that luxury. I want to appreciate what I do have. Like you say, I'm sure there will be other offers in the future.

LUKE: Good. I'm glad you have the right attitude to this. It was a vote of supreme confidence on Turner's part to offer you the job, so keep that in mind. If you really like her, maybe in the future when your year is up, she'll hire you for something else.

ALEXA: Maybe. We'll see. What's up with you?

LUKE: Going to meet with the PI about the issue we

discussed. More later. I'll be home for supper. I'll pick up some Ricardo Ribs on the way home.

ALEXA: Sounds perfect. The weather's nice. We can sit and watch the stars rise.

LUKE: Later. XO

ALEXA: Later. OX

I smiled and exhaled happily. Yes, I was sad that I couldn't accept the job offer, but at the same time, I was happy that I had it all — a loving husband, a healthy baby, loving parents, and was living in such a beautiful spot on the coast.

I knew that Luke was getting really concerned about the whole business with the brakes of the company car — the car that crashed and killed his parents when he and his sister were still just children. It brought up a whole scenario that wasn't one any child wanted to believe — that someone in his family business — maybe even his adoptive parents — arranged the deaths of his biological parents for the money.

Of the two Marshalls, I figured that Mrs. Marshall was the most likely culprit if the claim by the jailhouse snitch was true.

The problem was that often, inmates shared intel they received in prison for a lighter sentence or earlier release, and it was often doubtful if the intel was real or just a convenient lie.

Until there was an investigation, it would remain an open question.

What would the Marshalls do once they learned that someone was accusing them of sabotaging the company car?

LATER, while Leif was in his chair after his noon feed, I got a call from Candace, and smiled when I saw the call display.

"Hey, kiddo," she said, her voice ebullient as usual. "I was just going to take a ride out there for a visit. Are you available this afternoon? The weather's nice and I thought we could go for a walk along the beach."

"I'm all yours," I said. "Do you feel like ribs for supper? Luke can pick up extra. You like the coleslaw from Ricardo's, right?"

"Oh, yes. Yes. *Yes*. Please. Ricardo's Ribs are to die for. You sure you two lovebirds don't want to be alone or anything? I don't want to ruin your plans for the evening."

"Our plans for the evening will be exactly as follows: We'll eat, Luke will bathe Leif. I'll nurse him, Luke will put him to bed, and then Luke and I will either sit on the patio and watch the stars or collapse on the sofa and watch something on Netflix. You will be an enjoyable addition to the evening so please, stay overnight if you want. You could take the limo into the city in the morning."

"Nah, I have a car and I'll drive back when you yawn and kick me out."

"Okay, but the offer stands," I said. "There's always a bedroom for you if you want to stay."

"I know. I'll see you later."

"Bye," I said and ended the call. I turned to Leif. "Auntie Candy is coming for a visit."

Leif was busy squeezing and smooshing the soft toys on his tray, but he glanced up at me and smiled, responding to my happiness.

And I was happy.

I knew I'd made the right decision. I didn't want to miss any of Leif's days for the first year.

~

Candace arrived around two o'clock, driving a deep green Jeep. I stood on the steps and watched her get out of it, removing a bag from the back seat.

"You got a Jeep? Is it a rental or something?"

"You are looking at the proud new owner of a Jeep Wrangler Sport." She held out her hand, pretending to be a showroom model. "Check out the Sarge green color. It has all the bells and whistles."

"It's gorgeous," I replied, laughing at Candace's enthusiasm.

"It's my first car, sweets," she said and ran her hand over the hood. "I call him Sarge, and I love every inch of Sarge. I should because it's costing me a small fortune to park him."

"He's handsome. Come in and have some hot tea, or would you rather we spend some more time admiring Sarge?"

"Hot tea sounds perfect," she said and carried the bag into the house behind me.

"How's my little man?" she said and placed the bag down, holding out her arms to Leif. "How's the little Viking?"

I handed Leif to her and smiled when I saw her kiss his head. "He's doing fine. He had the sniffles and a bit of a fever, but he seems better now."

"Oh, that's too bad. I guess you have to get used to that. Kids get every bug that comes along in the first few years."

"What's in the bag?" I asked, pointing to the paper bag with string handles.

"It's a present for Leif. Bring it into the living room."

I followed Candace into the living room, bag in hand.

S. E. LUND

We got seated on the sofas and Candace pointed to the bag. "Open it and see."

I did, reaching into the bag to pull out a wrapped present. "What is it?"

"It's his first Star Wars toy."

I unwrapped the present and saw that it was a stuffed Baby Yoda.

"Every kid needs a stuffed Baby Yoda, don't you think?" Candace asked.

"Oh, my God. Of course, they do," I said with a laugh.

"I saw it in the mall yesterday and knew that Auntie Candy had to buy it for my little man."

I removed the Baby Yoda toy out of the box and then handed it to them. Leif reached out for it, which was one of the milestones to look for with babies his age. Candace and Leif played with Baby Yoda for only a moment before it went into Leif's mouth.

Candace laughed out loud at that. "Every boy needs a Baby Yoda toy. I can't wait for him to watch his first Star Wars movie."

I smiled and watched them together, glad that I had a best friend who was as excited about my baby as I could have hoped. For the next couple of hours, we sat and shared Leif between the two of us, and then, when it was time for his afternoon feed and nap, Candace insisted on burping Leif. She walked around the room with Leif on her shoulder and patted his back. When he finally let out a big burp, we both smiled.

"Good job!" Candace said and wiped his mouth off with the receiving blanket.

"Yes, he has a very good burp," I replied. Then, I took him from her, changed him and put him down for his afternoon nap.

I closed the door to his room, and then went downstairs and spent the rest of the afternoon with Candace, talking about the job offer and refusal, and about what was going on with Luke and the intrigue around the merger with Hanson.

"I'm so glad you said no, and that Luke said no to Hanson. I can't imagine losing you guys. I mean, I know you will probably leave at some point, but not so soon…"

"Me as well," I replied.

I was glad. I couldn't imagine upending my life and leaving, for either Houston or Brussels.

There would be time for that in the future.

I wanted to appreciate what I had here and now, and I intended to do just that.

CHAPTER 17

Luke

MY DAY PROCEEDED SMOOTHLY FOR THE FIRST COUPLE of hours, during which I spent catching up on business that had transpired since my last trip to town. Time passed quickly, and when lunch came, I checked my watch.

Time to meet John and go over the numbers Hanson provided to see what was really going on.

We met at a local diner that we both liked for the old-fashioned cheeseburgers and hand-cut fries. John was a big fan of Supernatural and fancied himself another Dean Winchester, with his love of diner bacon cheeseburgers.

John brought with him the file with all the financial info from Hanson Inc. Together, we spent the hour going over the numbers, trying to decide what it really meant and what Hanson wanted with Astra.

"What I suspect is that he wants to buy up all the competition so he can go his own way and not have to worry about anyone undercutting him on prices and suppliers or winning contracts," John concluded once we were finished reviewing the offer. "That's it. We get positions on the board, but those positions are largely symbolic. Hanson keeps control over the major decisions and directions the corporation takes."

I sighed. It wasn't what I wanted.

"I want to be the head of my own aerospace corporation, and work with other like-minded CEOs in joint ventures. Size is a virtue when it comes to such a huge venture as the space industry and making it work as a business, but I can't accept the idea of starting Astra and then losing control of it so soon after we just got off the ground."

"Look," John said, frowning. "It's either we buy out our competition or they buy us out. In aerospace, there are only a few big players."

"I want to become a big player," I said, firmly. "We haven't even had time to grow, let alone really compete with the big guys. This would stop that potential in its tracks."

John shrugged. "It's the way of the business world."

"You're okay with the deal?"

He leaned back and placed his napkin on the table. "I don't know, Luke. It's a lot of money. A lot. With it, you could spend the rest of your life sailing around the world."

"I could already do that," I replied. "If I really wanted. I don't. I want to grow Astra into a big player. That will take years, but this," I said and pointed to the file on the table between us. "This is the end of Astra and just another bump in assets for Hanson."

"I agree," John said. "We still had to consider it seriously."

"I have considered it seriously. Now that I see the offer in print, I know it's the wrong choice. For me."

"You should know Hanson offered me a plum executive position at the aerospace division and a pretty sweet offer of stock options."

"What?" I glanced up in shock and looked in John's eyes. "He did?"

John shrugged. "I guess he figured I was the weak link in the chain and could talk you into signing."

"Are you taking the job?"

"Nah," John said and adjusted his tie. "Not me. Astra all the way, baby. I just wanted to test you, see what you really wanted."

I sighed and leaned back, shaking my head. "You had me worried there for a moment. This is what I really want. I want to keep control of Astra. To hell with Hanson's big deal."

"I agree," John replied. We held up our soda glasses and toasted each other. "To Astra."

"To Astra," I replied. "Hanson isn't really as interested in aerospace as he is in acquisition and growth. Once he absorbed Astra and took control of its assets, he'd move on to some other acquisition. That's his game."

John nodded. "What's up with you for the rest of the afternoon? You said you had a meeting with the PI?"

"Yes, I have an appointment to meet with Brian George at two o'clock on the boardwalk just past the entrance closest to Astra's offices," I said. "I'll go back to the office with you, pick up a coffee at Jerome's and walk to the board-walk, find a spot and take a seat. Brian will find me and come over."

"Sounds really clandestine," John replied, wagging his eyebrows.

"It is. Brian figures there are people who might not like the information he knows and wants to keep it quiet."

"Why not meet somewhere private?"

"He's a former detective. I figure he knows what he's doing."

"Let me know what you learn," John said and grabbed the check. "If you can, that is."

"I will," I said and followed him to the counter where he paid for our meal.

We walked back to the building, which was just a couple of blocks away and went back into our respective offices.

I didn't really like all the cloak and dagger stuff with the meeting, but Brian thought it would be best. Given the intrigue of the past year, both with Eric and Blaine, I was willing to be cautious.

AT ONE FORTY-FIVE, I left the office, briefcase in tow, and went to Jerome's to pick up my afternoon coffee. Once I was finished paying, I took the sidewalk to the boardwalk along the river and found the closest empty bench. There was no one around, and just the occasional skateboarder or pedestrian. There were no strange men leaning against fenceposts reading newspapers nearby, so I figured we were out of earshot of anyone who might want to spy on us.

I felt ridiculous even thinking that, but if Brian felt a need to be extra cautious, I knew I should be as well.

About ten minutes later, a tall man with dark hair, shot through with grey, dark sunglasses and a beige trench coat took a seat beside me. He pulled out a newspaper and opened it up, then proceeded to look like he was reading intently.

"Mr. Luke Marshall," he said softly. He smiled as he spoke, without looking at me.

"Mr. Brian George, of Brian George Investigations, I presume?"

"The very one. Thanks for meeting me. Sorry about the need to meet in the open, but I don't want anyone nearby to hear us. Please turn off your cell and remove the SIM card. I've already done mine."

"Really?" I said, taking out my cell and removing the card from its slot. "You're that worried?"

"You're a very wealthy man, Mr. Marshall," he said. "That makes you a target."

I held up my hand to stop him. "Please call me Luke, and there are a lot wealthier men than me out there."

"Luke. If what I recently discovered about the accident that killed your parents is true, there are people who might not want me to talk to you."

"Please, tell me more," I said. "Won't we look strange sitting beside each other, talking? Isn't that enough to draw people's attention to us if they're following either of us?"

"If people know about this and are following us, I don't want them listening to what we talk about."

"You're the expert."

"I am," he said. "I spoke to a colleague in the FBI and called in a favor. He was able to access records from the garage that did the repair work on the company vehicle. He searched the files, which were in storage in a warehouse near the waterfront."

"It was almost twenty years ago. I'm surprised there are still records."

"Lucky for us, the FBI keeps records from the investigation for one hundred and ten years."

"Why was the FBI involved?" I asked, still curious.

"There was a short time when the accident investigator thought there might have been foul play involved, and so he sent the records to the FBI because the accident occurred across state lines in New Jersey and there was a thought that organized crime was involved."

I shook my head. "Wow. I had no idea that the FBI had been involved and that there was even a question about the accident. I thought it was quickly ruled accidental and the case was closed."

"That's the story, but believe me, it's not what really happened."

"What do you mean?" I asked, hearing a hint of conspiracy in his tone.

"I have a feeling that some of your father's moral right-eousness got him killed."

I frowned. "I don't understand what you mean, moral righteousness. Please — enlighten me."

Brian took in a breath, and folded his paper, glancing out over the waterfront. "There's a lot of mobbed up busi-ness here and in New Jersey."

"Yes, I'm well aware. My father's company wasn't involved in any of it."

"At the time, no, but since then, Marshall Inc., has been getting involved in the industries that are typically mobbed-up. Your father was a roadblock to that involvement."

I checked my watch, trying to hide my surprise at what he said. I glanced to my left, wondering if anyone was within earshot who might overhear what Brian was saying. "You mean, Marshall Inc., is now involved in it?"

"That's what I'm saying. They're keeping it at arm's-length, but they are definitely involved through a series of numbered companies, so the main business appears clean. It's typical for industries involved with the Mafia."

"Russian or Italian?"

"And Irish. Don't forget my people. We had a bigger presence back in the 20th Century, but the Russians have become a much bigger player, and believe me, they are not nice people."

"How do you mean?"

"Well, the Irish would stick a gun in your mouth and shoot you, but the Russians?" He turned to me and met my eyes. "The Russians skin you alive, cut off your balls and dick and shove them down your throat so that you choke to death on them. That's how I mean."

"Jesus..."

"Yeah, Mary and Joseph, too. They are, and pardon my French, nasty motherfuckers. The Italian Mafia had rules at least. You do not want to mess with the Russian Mafia."

"No, I most certainly don't. So, you think the Russian Mafia put a hit on my parents?"

"I think someone wanted your father out of the way so that he wouldn't keep putting a brake on working with them, yeah. The question is who."

"You have any ideas? My stepfather? My stepmother?"

Brian shrugged. "That is the question. The other question is why the accident was so quickly ruled accidental. Who was paid off and why? What were the FBI doing? Why did they quickly shut down the case?"

"You have any theories?"

Brian exhaled heavily and shook his head. "This is just a theory, okay? I'm wondering if it was more valuable to them to have it look like an accident rather than prosecute those who might have been involved. You understand what I'm saying?"

I frowned. "You mean, the FBI wanted the business deals with the Russian Mafia to go through and so they looked the other way? Didn't pursue the case?" My blood started to boil at the implications. I turned to Brian. "Is that what your working hypothesis is?"

Brian shrugged. "It's a hunch. Look, I've been involved in some cases before where the Feds were involved. Sometimes, they let certain crimes slide so that they can try to catch the bigger fish."

"What's bigger than a double murder?"

"Getting intel on the Russian Mafia so that you can go in and arrest the big cheeses?"

"Isn't murder big enough to arrest them?"

He shook his head. "If there were no links or proof that anyone in the upper echelons ordered the hit, they couldn't arrest anyone but the lower-level types. If they want the big cheese, they have to wait for the right evidence."

"Has that happened?"

"No." Brian shook his head. "Like I say, this is all just a hunch on my part, but when I learned the FBI was involved, and the accident happened in Jersey, I right away thought Mafia. That would be where I focused my inquiries if you want me to continue."

I sighed heavily. "That is definitely what I want you to do," I said. "All this time, I've thought my parents were victim of a bad accident on the freeway. It happens all the time. Now, I have to start thinking that they were killed to further a deal, and the FBI looked the other way so they could wait and get the big bosses? You have to understand I'm both skeptical and horrified."

"I understand," Brian said, nodding. "Believe me. I understand. I'll do some more digging and get back to you with anything I uncover. But you should know that I have to be really careful. I don't want anyone to know we're digging. Even this far out from the crime, there would be people who want to keep it covered up. Both among the Feds and those directly involved in ordering the hit and who benefitted from it."

"You mean my stepparents."

"Them, too. If they were involved, you can imagine they would want it to stay quiet. There is no statute of limitations on murder."

"Good. Whoever ordered my parent's murders, I want them prosecuted."

Brian stood up and adjusted his hat. "I'll keep digging."

"Thank you."

With that, Brian walked off north along the boardwalk. On my part, I sat on the bench, staring off over the Hudson, and wondered what the hell we had uncovered and what the consequences would be if we discovered the truth.

My cell rang. I checked the call display and saw that it was Alexa.

"Hey, babe," I said, smiling to myself at the thought of her with Leif. "What's up?"

"Just calling to see how things are going. Candace is here and will probably stay the night. Can you bring extra ribs and everything so we can feed her as well?"

"I'd be happy to."

"Great. See you when you get here. Love you."

"Love you back."

I ended the call, smiling. At least I had Alexa and Leif. I might not be able to look my stepparents in the eye ever again if we learned they had been involved in the hit that killed my parents, but I had my own family now and I still had my sister Dana and her son little James.

That was all I really needed.

CHAPTER 18

Alexa

CANDACE AND I SPENT THE AFTERNOON JUST THE WAY I wanted. We walked along the beach, then sat on the patio under the awning and watched the waves while Leif sat on Candace's lap, played in his playpen, or napped.

We blabbed the entire time, which was a welcome change from spending time alone while Luke was in town. I caught up with her hijinks at her new job, and even dragged out of her the details of her burgeoning romance with the Wall Street cutie, Nate.

"Come on," I said and pushed her playfully. "You must have loads of pics of him. Show me."

She smiled while she pulled up some images on her cell. Then, she handed the cell to me. I scrolled through them, noting the jet-black hair, the square jaw, the right amount of scruff and the very blue eyes.

"Wow, he's a hunk of man flesh," I said, remembering her own description of Luke back when we first met.

"That he is," she said with a satisfied sigh. "I'm so lucky. He's dashing. He's an up-and-coming trader for a big investment company. He wants to go into day trading and be his own boss. I guess he's really good at it and is building up quite a portfolio."

"Lucky you," I said with a smile to match her own. "That jaw..."

"You should see the rest of him. Mama Mia..." She licked her lips and we both laughed.

"Bring him out here some weekend for some sun and surf. I'll get a chance to see him in his swim trunks."

"You name the weekend. We'll be out here."

"Deal."

"So, it's getting serious, is it?"

"Well, we're long past the ten-date threshold, and we're into our first months of being exclusive, if that's what you mean."

"That's what I mean."

"It's still early days, and I don't want to get ahead of myself, but yeah. We click. We feel right. We want the same things out of life. Mostly getting a nice place in Brooklyn and living the dream. He wants to travel as much as possible, which is why he wants to be a day trader. He can work at home or work wherever there's an internet connection so he can trade online. He wants to take a trip across Europe. Ride the Orient Express..."

"Sounds like fun and just the right kind of nerdy hunk you need."

"Yes, and he wants to go to Norway and Iceland and watch the Northern Lights. Can you believe it? He's going to be rich and he's a nerd and he's a hunk of man flesh. How did I get so lucky?"

"Don't sell yourself short, girl. You're very sexy, and you have a killer brain."

Candace fluffed her curls and tilted her head coyly. "Ya think?"

She made kissing noises and puckered her lips seductively. Then she laughed out loud.

"He likes the fact I'm a science geek. Can you believe that? Most men I meet are intimidated by my brain. Not Nate. He's smart enough that he thinks I'm right for him. No toxic masculinity. No fragile masculinity either."

I reached over and squeezed her hand. "I'm glad for you. We're both lucky."

"We are," she said and squeezed my hand back.

For the rest of the afternoon, we enjoyed the breeze and the sun, waiting for Luke to return with our ribs for dinner.

Finally, at around six in the evening, Luke arrived, bags filled with Ricardo's Ribs in hand.

He held them up in the air when I went to meet him at the front entrance.

"Here they are," he said and handed them to me, while he leaned over and gave me a warm kiss. "I know this is what you're really waiting for. I'm just along for the ride."

"As long as you know your place," I said with a smile and took the ribs into the kitchen. Candace was waiting at the kitchen island with Leif in her arms.

"There's your daddy," she said and waved one of Leif's tiny arms in the air. "Say 'Hi, daddy!'"

"Hey, Candace," Luke said and gave her a smile. He went over and picked up Leif, giving him a kiss. On his part Leif seemed happy and tried to bite Luke on the chin.

Everything — simply everything — went into his mouth now. Hands, toys, people's chins and faces.

"Hey, there little mister. How have you been for Mommy and Auntie Candy?"

"He's been a little doll," Candace replied. "I hope I get one as good as him when I have babies."

"We are lucky," Luke said and took a seat beside Candace, Leif in his arms. "He sleeps well and eats well. No complaints. We're acclimatized to being parents, I think."

Luke glanced at me, and I nodded. "I think we have the parenting thing down by now."

"Good," Candace said. "What's new in the aerospace industry? Alexa told me that you have a potentially big deal with some unnamed but very powerful player."

"That we do," Luke said and took in a deep breath. I handed him a bottle of his favorite craft beer out of the refrigerator, and he happily took it and drank down a long sip. "There are a few complications, and we don't think we're going to go forward with the deal."

"Oh, that's too bad," Candace said with a pout.

"No, not really. It would mean the end of Astra and we'd just become another cog in a much bigger wheel. That was never the vision I had for Astra. I want to retain control over it and grow it, partner with other players in a consortium, each of us with our own specialty. This deal would mean we would be swallowed up into the larger company and would lose control. It's not for us."

"You two made your decision?" I said, going to the stove and putting the ribs in to keep them hot until we were ready to eat.

"We did," Luke replied. "The CEO offered John a plum position and stock options to try to get him to convince me to accept the offer but we both agreed it wasn't what either of us wanted for Astra. So, no go."

I nodded and sipped my glass of soda. "Too bad, but if it's not what you want, it's not a good deal, no matter how big it is."

"Agreed."

I watched Luke take a big sip of his beer and then he exhaled like he was still disappointed that the deal fell through. Or, that he had to reject the deal.

"There'll be others," I said and held out my glass of soda for a toast. "To Astra. May it find bigger and better partners in the future."

"Real partners," Luke added. "Not the kind that want to swallow you up, absorb your assets, and then spit out what they don't like."

"Hear hear," Candace said.

We all toasted Astra and then prepared for our supper of ribs, seasoned fries and coleslaw.

All in all, it was a lovely dinner and evening. We took turns holding Leif on our laps and then, after Luke gave Leif a bath, I fed Leif and put him down for the night.

Candace stood in the doorway and watched the crib, smiling at the stars circling on the ceiling overhead and the rocket mobile.

"What a great nursery," she said. "That kid will grow up to be an astronaut."

WE WENT BACK to the patio, and I placed the baby monitor on the table beside my reclining lawn chair. Together, the three of us watched the stars rise and enjoyed the evening.

"I had other news today," Luke said, his voice sounding conspiratorial.

"Oh, do tell," I said and turned to him. "More about the accident? You met with the PI, right?"

"What accident?" Candace frowned.

I turned to Luke. "I haven't told Candace the details yet, wanting to talk to you first about whether I should."

"It's about my parent's deaths," Luke replied. "You can tell her."

"There's a PI?" Candace turned to me, her eyes wide. "What's going on?"

I took in a deep breath. "Luke was contacted by a private investigator who is looking into the deaths and thinks it might not have been an accident."

Beside me, Luke exhaled heavily. I could tell that he was troubled by what he'd learned during his meeting with the PI earlier in the day.

"The PI says that the FBI were briefly involved in the case, because the man in the other vehicle was apparently a mafia heavy. At first, they thought it might not have been an accident and that the man might have targeted my parents," Luke said. "But they got out of the case soon after, and ruled it was accidental. My PI thinks it wasn't."

"Wow — the FBI were involved? So, they initially thought he might have what — run them off the road?"

"As far as I know. A witness said that it appeared that the two cars collided when the mafia guy's car passed my parents. Since he was connected to a business in direct competition with my father's company, they thought it was a hit."

"You think your family's company was mobbed up?" Candace asked, her eyes wide.

Luke shrugged. "No. The opposite. The fact that they

weren't going along with the mob might have been a reason why they were targeted. Maybe one of the executives was mobbed up and the FBI was interested in the crash because of that." Luke turned to Candace, his voice solemn. "This can't leave this room, okay? If it is what my PI thinks, it might be that there were some mafia ties and that was why my parents were killed."

"Oh, my God," Candace said, covering her mouth with a hand. "That's horrible. I'm so sorry."

Luke shrugged. "The big question is, who set it up? An inmate who has terminal cancer and wants to repent says that he tampered with the brake line, thinking it was a simple insurance fraud case. He never imagined that it would result in a crash that killed two people."

"What did he think would happen when the brake line was punctured?" Candace said, her voice incredulous. "Of course, the brakes would fail, and the car would crash."

"Especially if another vehicle was trying to run theirs off the road. The inmate said he thought it was just so they could get insurance for the vehicle. You know, write off the cost of a new car or something. Thing is, he didn't question. He just did it for the money."

Candace shook her head. "I dunno. I've watched enough crime shows to know that cops don't look on jail-house confessions very well. I mean, they have incentive to lie in order to get their sentences reduced. Why come forward now?"

Luke shrugged. "Because he's sick and dying so he wanted to come clean about his past crimes."

I reached over and took Luke's hand. This had to be really upsetting for him — to learn so long after the fact that his parents were murdered?

That the mafia was involved?

And worst of all, how were the Marshalls involved?

"So, who ordered the hit?" Candace asked. "Who paid to have the brake line damaged?"

"That is the question," Luke replied. "I don't like some of the options. The police usually look at who has the most to gain from a murder when they look for suspects. The two people who had the most to gain were my stepparents. And the Mob if they could use them to get leverage with the business."

Candace shook her head. "I'm so sorry, Luke. I don't know what to say. Maybe it was someone else in the executive who wanted to work with the Mob and who cooperated. But why did the FBI get out of the case?"

"That's question number two. Why did they get out?"

"Any theories?" I asked.

Luke shook his head. "My PI says that there's no excuse, unless they never really did get out."

"What do you mean?" Candace leaned forward.

"Maybe they were working with the Marshalls to get at bigger fish in the Mafia that runs the ports in New Jersey and New York. I don't know, but I'm paying him to do his best to find out."

I sighed. "You may not like the answer."

"I'm preparing myself for any eventuality," Luke said and kissed my knuckles.

I smiled and nodded in response.

What else could I say? I'd read before about people getting away with murder so that the FBI could go after bigger fish.

It was a cruel reality that sometimes, that was the way the world worked.

For Luke's sake, I hope that wasn't the case but only time would tell.

CHAPTER 19

Luke

FOR THE REST OF THE WEEK, I WAITED WITH MY CELL in hand for some more news from either Ken Hanson or Brian George but received word from neither.

I assumed that the deal with Hanson was finished, and merely expected that we would hear no more about it, since being swallowed up by Hanson Inc., was a deal breaker for me, not to mention moving to Houston.

When John called on Thursday afternoon while Leif and Alexa were both snoozing, I expected he had the same notion, but instead, he dropped a bombshell on me.

"He really wants the deal," John said. "He's come back with a different offer. This time, both your objections are taken care of."

"What?" I frowned. "He doesn't want us or Seneca to merge with Hanson Inc.?"

"No. That's no longer in the agreement. He agreed that

we will set up a separate entity, and each of us contributes to that entity our share of the project. Independently run from Hanson Inc., Seneca and Astra. Also, the head office could be located in Houston, as he wished, and you and Adam would appoint someone as co-CEO of the new venture, he would appoint someone from Hanson. You could each stay in your respective coasts. Adam on the West, you on the East and Hanson in Texas."

"Wow," I said and took in a deep breath, rubbing my forehead as I considered. "He must really want to work with us."

"He must really," John replied. "Does this satisfy your main objections?"

"I guess. What about other funders? Would they come in as minor players? With Hanson's money, we really don't need anyone else."

"No, you wouldn't. Hanson's the whale to your and Seneca's dolphins. Even Campbell is small potatoes compared to Hanson."

"I prefer to be seen as a killer whale, actually," I said with a laugh, a weight taken off my shoulders now that Hanson had decided to cooperate instead of co-opt Astra.

"Hanson said he was testing Astra's and Seneca's resolve to see how committed you both were to staying at the head of your companies. If you really didn't have the vision and drive to stay at the helm, he would be happy to take Astra and Seneca over in a buy-out. Otherwise, he would be happy to do a joint venture."

"That's great," I said, nodding in understanding. "He wanted to know how committed we were to the vision and whether he could buy us, in other words."

"Yes," John replied. "Either way, he gets to work with

Astra and Seneca either as the new majority owner or as a co-founder of the joint venture."

"He likes us," I said, feeling silly, but repeating the gif of Sally Field when accepting the Oscar for her performance. "He really likes us."

"He does," John said, sounding amused. "He really likes us."

We both laughed.

"Don't tell him I said that," I added.

"No way," John replied. "Come on — it's a classic response. I have to use it in the staff meeting to announce the joint venture."

"You'll do no such thing," I said, unable to keep from smiling.

"Okay, I'll tell you what I'm gonna do. I'm gonna send a gif around with your face superimposed on Sally Field's."

"You do and I will retaliate."

"I can't wait," John said with a good-natured laugh.

We discussed meeting the next day to go over the paperwork that Hanson promised to provide.

"We'll meet with Hanson, Adam, Frank and Jack on Saturday night for a celebratory meal. Hanson insisted."

"I guess we should start calling him Ken if we're going to enter into a joint venture. What does Adam think of this? He's happy, right?"

"He is, as is Jack Tate and Frank Campbell. They want to be part of the consortium and not sell to Hanson."

"Good, good," I said and leaned back in my chair, running a hand through my hair with relief. "Wow. This is really more than I hoped for. I wanted to see several big players create a consortium to go to the asteroid belt. It'll take something really big and really rich to fund such a

S. E. LUND

venture. There is no way Astra could do it on our own, so this is what we need."

"He's going to want to have a big part in it," John said.

"As he should, given he's the whale. Who else do you think will get involved?"

"Hanson — Ken — has some ideas and contacts in the industry. He'll be the one to arrange that."

"Great," I said. "I'll come into the city tomorrow for the morning and we can meet and go over everything. Get ready for Saturday."

"You two will be able to come into the city for the night?"

"Yes, we can get the Dixons to come out and stay with Leif. No problem."

"Great. I'll see you tomorrow."

"Tomorrow," I replied and ended the call.

I actually jumped up and pumped my fist, I was so excited. I poked my head into the bedroom where Alexa and Leif were sleeping and realized I didn't want to wake either of them, so instead, I went downstairs, slipped on my running shoes, and spoke with the guard who was in charge of security for the property. I let him know I was going for a run, and he sent one of the guards to watch me. A car would drive along the road bordering the beach while I ran the beach itself. That way, they could keep an eye on me. In case someone with bad intent was lurking around the area.

I didn't think anyone was but had grown accustomed to the extra security.

After warming up, I ran along the beach to work off some of the excess energy I felt.

It was super — the response Hanson had to my refusal to accept the deal. He understood that I wanted to keep control of Astra and was willing to cooperate instead of swallow Astra up.

That suggested to me that he was actually committed to the project and not just out to make more acquisitions.

I couldn't be happier. He was the whale in the industry. If he created the new entity, it would attract even more investors and partners.

For the next fifteen minutes, I ran along the beach, enjoying the late afternoon sunlight, and working off some of the excess energy I felt from the news. When I arrived back at the beach house, I stood outside and had a shower at the outside shower stall, washing the sweat off and then I plopped down on a reclining chair on the patio, a glass of cold soda in hand, waiting for Alexa and Leif to wake up and join me.

Alexa joined me a few moments later. When I saw her, I stood up and went to her, taking her into my arms.

"I love you," I said and kissed her warmly.

She laughed and ran her fingers through my hair, smiling up at me. "What's got into you? An unprovoked I love you? What happened?"

"John called. Hanson wants the deal. I guess he was just testing me and Adam to see if we could be bought. When he learned neither Adam nor I could be, he agreed."

"Oh, my God, Luke," she said and smiled brightly. "That's amazing. What's in the deal?"

She sat beside me on the patio, and I gave her the details as John had related them.

"I'm going in tomorrow to meet with John and go over the papers, but I think we'll probably sign them," I said. "A consortium of private companies is exactly what I want. If we were to go public, or become part of Hanson, we would be required by law to put profit first, and not make the kind of investments we need in technological development. Private companies like Astra, Campbell, Seneca and Hanson can decide to forgo profit for a few years in return for some technological breakthroughs. If we were public, we'd have to make profit margins or lose investments. It's the law. I want us to stay private. I want this to be a joint venture of companies who are dedicated to developing the tech needed to mine the asteroid belt. It's going to take a lot of money and a lot of initial research and development. It's going to take a decade, but once it's done, the profits will be out of this world. So to speak," I said, and noticed Alexa was smiling at me indulgently.

"I'm so happy for you," she said and leaned across to me and kissed me.

Of course, it was at that moment, just when I was wondering if I could sneak her into our bedroom for a quick session of lovemaking that the little man made his presence known.

He squeaked on the baby monitor and Alexa laughed.

"I guess our plans will have to wait. Duty calls..."

"They can wait for Saturday night when we stay in the city. Can you call your parents and see if they're available to stay Saturday night so we can go into town? Hanson wants us all to meet and celebrate signing the papers."

"Of course," Alexa said. "I know they were hoping to come out this weekend. It will be perfect."

We kissed again.

"I'll go get Leif," I said and stood up. "Maybe you could make us some iced tea."

"Will do," Alexa said and followed me into the kitchen. I went upstairs to get Leif, opening the door to his room, which was dim, the constellations circling on the ceiling above him.

"There you are," I said and went to his crib. He smiled up at me and at that moment, I felt like life was absolutely perfect. I had a beautiful wife whom I loved with all my heart, a wonderful baby boy, who smiled up at me like a cherub, and was going to sign an amazing deal with one of the biggest whale investors in the aerospace industry.

I couldn't be happier.

WE WENT to bed early Thursday night, and I could tell that Alexa was just too tired after a long walk on the beach with Leif in a carrier to make love, so I thought of the deal and tried to put off my desire for at least forty-eight hours when we could be alone in the apartment in Manhattan. It took some time, but I finally fell asleep sometime after one in the morning. I woke when my watch alarm went off just after eight. Alexa was already up and was feeding Leif. I could hear her humming to him over the baby monitor on the bed beside me. I felt bad that I'd slept right through the nightly feed and now had slept through Alexa getting up to feed Leif. I had just been so tired and so relieved that the deal with Hanson was going to go through that I must have been totally unconscious.

I got up, had a quick shower, and then dressed in my usual business suit for the meeting with John. I didn't need to get all dressed up, but I wanted to be able to meet with the staff in the office and tell them the good news. I wanted to look like the successful space entrepreneur and so didn't want to disappoint.

I called the limo service and arranged for it to meet me outside. I had just enough time to get a cup of coffee and a bagel from the kitchen before it would arrive.

When I got downstairs, the caffeinated coffee pot was full and there was a thermos already filled with it waiting for me. Alexa came down the stairs with Leif in her arms.

"There you two are," I said and went over to meet them at the entrance to the kitchen. I took Leif from Alexa's arms and kissed his still-bald head. "I'm sorry I was such a neglectful daddy and slept through the night feed and this morning's, too."

"Don't worry," Alexa said and went to get her own cup of decaf from the one-cup coffee maker beside the main one. "We understood. You had great news yesterday and needed to sleep in. Leif and I will make sure Daddy makes up for it, won't we?" she said to Leif, who smiled at her, his pacifier in his mouth.

"I promise you I will make it up to you," I said to her. While I held Leif and watched, Alexa popped a bagel in the toaster. "Do you want a bagel to go? Cream cheese?"

"You're too good to me," I said and nodded.

She was too good to me, but I loved every minute of it. When my cell dinged indicating that the limo was outside, I went to the front entrance and slipped on my shoes. Alexa followed me with Leif in her arms, a bagel and coffee clutched in the other.

"Don't forget your briefcase," she said and motioned to the bottom of the staircase.

I kissed her and Leif, grabbed the coffee and bagel and briefcase, and left the house, ready to take on the day and look at the papers Hanson had sent over. Life was good.

Hell, it was more than good.

It was fantastic.

CHAPTER 20

Alexa

LEIF AND I SPENT THE MORNING DOING OUR USUAL routine, feeding, playing, walking along the beach, then when I put him down for his morning nap, I plopped down on the recliner on the patio and called my parents.

"Hey, are you two available for Saturday night babysitting? Luke's deal went through, and we are supposed to go into Manhattan for dinner and a celebration with the new partners."

"Of course, dear," my mother said excitedly. "We would have insisted if you hadn't asked. So, I thought the deal fell through?"

I spent the next few moments explaining what changed with the big deal Luke had been trying to negotiate with Hanson.

"That's so good to hear," she said, and I listened as she yelled at my father, who must have been out of the room.

"I'm putting you on speakerphone so he can talk to you as well. Just hold on."

"Hey, honey," my father said, and I could hear the excitement in his voice. "So, the big deal is still on after all?"

"Yes," I said. "Luke got exactly what he wanted — a consortium of private investors instead of being swallowed up by the whale."

We spent the next few minutes discussing the deal and the implications.

"This means you won't be moving to Houston, right? I couldn't stand the thought of you moving to Houston. It's so far from New York..."

"No, while the headquarters will be in Texas, Astra will remain in New York, Seneca in Washington, and Hanson will remain in Texas. All's right with the world. At least, according to Luke."

"That's great, honey. As long as Luke's happy, we're happy. How are you doing after turning Professor Turner down?"

I sighed. "I'm relieved. It was an exciting opportunity, but it's just bad timing. One day, I'll get the job I want, when the time is right. For now, I want to focus on Leif, and I want Luke to be involved with Leif during this first year or two."

"That's great," my mother said, and I knew she agreed with my decision. "You won't regret it. Children grow so fast, and before you know it, they're off to college, and you wonder where the time went. Enjoy this period of Leif's life. Cherish every moment."

"I plan to. Luke and I plan to."

We spoke for a few more minutes and she promised me that they would arrive in the afternoon on Saturday so that

Luke and I could take the limo into the city in time for our dinner with Hanson and the other investors.

I ended the call and then sat back on the deck chair and watched the surf on the beach below the property.

It was going to be another gorgeous day on the ocean, and I was happy to have the chance to enjoy it for a brief time alone while Leif slept.

It was while I was reading over my social media that I got a notification of an incoming email. I checked my inbox and there it was — the response from Professor Turner.

I felt bad as I tapped on the mail icon and opened the email.

Dear Alexa:

I completely understand your reluctance to leave your new baby so soon and move to Brussels, but my loss is your little one's gain. Don't worry about me — I have a few other candidates, but you were my top choice, so I figured I'd offer it to you first. I've got a tentative acceptance from another former student, so I'm good. In other news, I gave your name to a contact I have in the UN and said that if they were ever in need of a great candidate for any policy job, they should keep you in mind and I hope you don't mind, but I forwarded him your C.V. Hopefully, it will bear fruit for you some day. I think a recommendation from me will put you in a good position in the future, when you're ready to let your little one go into daycare.

Keep in touch and I'll let you know how the new position in Brussels goes.

Cheers,

Helen

I was really glad to know that she wasn't angry with me for turning down the plum first job with her and that she understood why. I figured it would be easy enough for her to find someone else for the position and I was right. It made me all warm inside to know she sent my C.V., to someone she knew in the UN. It would be nice to be headhunted instead of having to go out and look for work.

I wrote her back right away.

Dear Helen,

Thanks so much for the reply and for the recommendation. I'm glad you have found another candidate for the job. It's such an exciting opportunity. I would have loved to accept it at a better time in my life and I'm glad you understood my reasons for turning the offer down. It had nothing to do with you or the opportunity, which are both amazing, and has everything to do with little Leif. Thanks for sending my C.V. off to your contact in the UN. Maybe someday I can work for them. It would be a dream come true.

All the best.

Alexa

I smiled as I sent the email, glad that I had such a great person looking out for me.

LEIF WOKE up just before lunch, so I went to get him, and nursed him right away. After changing him, I took him downstairs and prepared my own lunch. I figured some avocado toast and fruit salad would be a good option. I had still a dozen pounds on me above my pre-baby weight and wanted to lose a few pounds over the next couple of months. Nothing too drastic — I wasn't going to fret about it. Luke even joked that he liked my very nicely rounded butt and breasts just fine and not to even think about losing weight, but I didn't want to take too long to get back to my pre-baby weight and physique. I knew Luke loved me just the way I was, but I wanted to be back to normal when I finished nursing Leif, whenever that was.

It was as I was sitting on the patio, enjoying my fruit salad that I saw a man come running up the beach towards the beach house. I frowned when I saw him for it was one of the security guards from the security company. He was wearing a business suit and had his hand to his ear. I recognized him as Jeb. He'd worked for the company for the past couple of months and was a tall beast of a man with a shaved head and big meaty hands. Luke had said he was former military.

"Sorry, Ma'am, but could you bring your baby inside, please? Right away, thanks."

I jumped up right away, not wanting to argue, and grabbed Leif from his place on his stomach in his playpen.

I rushed inside and the guard closed the sliding door behind me.

"What's the matter?"

"There was an incident on the road approaching the house," the man said. "A man fled the vehicle and ran to the beach. I wanted to make sure you were inside and safe just in case he was a person of interest to us. It may turn out to be just a local thug who didn't want to answer questions from the police, but to be safe, I want you to stay inside until we get the all-clear."

"Of course," I said and sat with Leif in the living room, my heart pounding. "What happened? What kind of incident?"

"One of our guards noticed the vehicle was driving very slowly past the house several times, and so we called the local police to check them out. The plates returned that they were stolen, and so the police gave chase. The vehicle went into a ditch a few houses down the beach and the suspects fled the scene. Police gave chase and caught one of the two, but the other man has not been apprehended. They're currently doing a door-to-door to check for the other suspect. That's all I have so far."

I swallowed back my fear, figuring that it was probably just a couple of local kids who were casing the houses, looking for an empty place that they could break into and steal from. Several of the homes along the coast near us were empty most of the year. The owners were wealthy people who lived in the city and only came out during the peak season in the summer. Now that it was September, and school was returning, the summer inhabitants had fled to the city, and we were among the few who remained.

"Probably just some local hoods trying to find an unoccupied house to loot," Jeb said, standing at the patio door, his legs spread, his hands behind his back.

"Probably," I said and forced a smile. "I understand most of the houses along the coast are empty once September comes and people go back to the city."

"That's what I understand as well," Jeb replied.

I didn't know what to do, so I switched on the flatscreen and watched the local news while Leif played on the carpet with his toys.

I heard my cell chime and checked the display. It was a call from Luke.

"Hey," I said when I answered.

"Are you okay? I just got a call from the security service that there was an incident close to the beach house and that they had you in lockdown."

"They called you?"

"Yes," Luke said, his voice sounding concerned. "I'm on my way back right now, but we're twenty minutes out. How are you?"

"I'm fine," I said, exhaling now that I knew Luke was almost home. "We're both fine. Jeb is standing guard at the sliding doors and the police are doing a door-to-door to look for the other suspect, who fled on foot."

"Good. I'm glad I hired them. It makes me feel a lot more secure leaving you and coming into the city knowing that there are three guards watching over you and the beach house property."

"Me, too," I said and sighed. "See you when you get here."

"I love you," Luke said, his voice warm and deep.

"I love you back," I said and smiled. I ended the call and glanced at Leif, who was shoving a light green toy into his mouth. It was the Baby Yoda that Candace gave him earlier in the week.

I tried to calm myself as I waited for Luke to return from his trip into the city to meet with John. He would have some good news to report, and so I wanted our night together to be relaxed and happy.

"There he goes," Jeb said and opened the sliding door. I stood up and glanced outside. Sure enough, some young man dressed in a black hoodie and jeans was hightailing it down the beach. A cop in a black uniform ran after him. It looked like both were struggling. Running in the sand wasn't always the easiest, and as we watched, the two ran out of sight.

"You stay here, Ma'am," Jeb said and left the house, closing the sliding door behind him. He went to stand at the end of the yard, watching the beach. I wanted to go out and join him, maybe watch the takedown, but stayed where I was as he commanded.

As I watched, Jeb put his hand to his ear and spoke.

Then, he came back to the patio and opened the sliding door.

"The bad guy is in police custody," Jeb said, a smile on his face. "Preliminary thoughts are that they are some local hoods cruising for a place to break into and not a person of interest to you and Mr. Marshall personally."

I nodded and went back to the living room and the sofa, glad that that was over.

I knew exactly what he meant by a 'person of interest' to me or Luke.

Eric or Blaine.

I was hopeful that Eric was no longer a threat to us, at least physically, but Blaine was and as long as he was free, we had to stay on guard.

CHAPTER 21

Luke

WHEN I GOT THE CALL FROM THE SECURITY COMPANY, my heart started to race.

Of course, something would happen the one day of the week when I was away from the house...

"What's the matter?"

"Sir, we had a report of a pursuit of a stolen car in the area near your house and that police had given chase and had one suspect in custody but the other suspect was at large. As a precaution, we've locked down the house and one of our guards in presently with your wife to ensure her safety just in case. We have no reason to think this is in any way connected to you or Mrs. Marshall, but on the off chance that it is, we decided to take steps to protect her and the property."

"Thanks for calling me. We're about twenty minutes away. I'll stop in and speak to you when I arrive."

"Understood," he said, and we ended the call.

Immediately, I called Alexa to see how she was doing. This would upset her, of course, and even though it probably had nothing to do with Alexa, it would be a reminder that she was in danger from Blaine.

After speaking with her, I ended the call, glad that she sounded fine and that she felt safe with the guard watching over her and Leif.

While we drove towards Westhampton and the beach house, I thought about the whole business with Blaine and how terrible it was that he was granted bail.

He was a smart and slippery man and an ongoing threat to Alexa as long as he was free.

We finally drove along the road that led to the beach house property, and I wanted to stop and speak with police, who were parked on the side of the road near the vehicle that had gone into the ditch. The lights were flashing, and several uniformed police officers were standing next to a police car. I could see that someone was seated in the back seat of the sedan. In another vehicle, there looked to be another man in the rear seat.

It must be the two suspects.

"Stop here," I said to the driver. He complied and I got out of the limo and walked over to the police officers, who were standing off to the side of the road.

"Hello, I'm Luke Marshall, owner of the house next door. Can you give me an update on the situation?"

I shook hands with one of the senior police officers, Officer Gus Simmons, a forties heavy-set man with greying hair and moustache. He pushed his cap back and glanced over the vehicle in the ditch.

"One of your guards, actually, noticed the vehicle had been driving back and forth in front of the property and called us with the plates. We checked and they're registered to a stolen vehicle from Queens, so we sent a patrol car to check it out. A chase ensued and the vehicle went off the road there. The two suspects fled the scene, my officers gave chase and we've apprehended them both. They'll be taken into custody and booked."

"Any ID?"

"They're both from Queens and apparently stole the vehicle and took a joyride out to Fire Island and were looking for a place to park so they could go to the beach. I see nothing in their possession to cast doubt on that story. Neither of them has a record beyond impaired driving, so I think they're the real thing."

"That's good to know," I said and glanced at the one suspect, who was sulking in the back of the police car. His long hair was hanging in his eyes, and he looked very sullen. Probably just what the officer said - two young men joyriding and hoping for an afternoon on the beach. Nothing more.

"Thanks for the update," I said and shook hands with Simmons again. Then, I glanced at the vehicle and back at the two suspects before getting back in the limo for the rest of the way to the beach house.

I spoke briefly with the guard on duty at the gates, and then, I went inside.

Alexa and Leif were in the living room and there was a guard, whom I assumed was Jeb, standing at the sliding doors, his back to the room.

"Hey, you two," I said and went directly to Alexa and picked up Leif from her arms. I kissed his head and then kissed her when she stood up from the sofa. "How are you? I spoke with police, and they think the two stole the vehicle from Queens and were just joyriding."

"I'm fine, other than a bit of a scare. Why were they driving back and forth in front of the house?"

"Police think they were looking for some place to park so they could go to the beach. It was just a coincidence that they went off the road near our place. Nothing to worry about. Neither of the guys have records beyond some petty stuff like impaired driving so they weren't hired hitmen sent to take us out."

I smiled and watched as Alexa smiled slowly. "That's good to know," she said and exhaled. "I just wish they'd put him away for a good long time, so I didn't have to worry."

"The PI is looking into it for us," I said and stroked Alexa's hair. "If you want, we could put a tail on him, but it would be a very costly venture. You'd need at least six men on payroll, one for each eight-hour shift and then to cover weekends. That works out to quite a cost."

"It's not worth it," Alexa said, her brow furrowed. "We have great security on the beach house," she said and pointed around the house to the security cameras, the security system in the property, and to Jeb, the security guard. "We'll always be protected. Every single minute. We don't have to worry."

"If you're sure," I said and pulled her into my arms and held them both, Leif on one shoulder and Alexa on the other.

My little family...

I made eye contact with Jeb, and he nodded and went to stand outside on the patio, giving Alexa and I some privacy.

We sat on the sofa and Alexa sat next to me while I held Leif on my lap.

"How's my little man?" I said and handed him the stuffed Baby Yoda, which he promptly jammed into his mouth. "Did you remain unaware through all the commotion?"

Alexa finally smiled and focused her attention back onto Leif. "He did, of course. He was playing in his playpen and never once made a fuss. Jeb came and told me to go inside as a precaution, so we came in here and waited."

"See? There's nothing to worry about. There will always be someone in the yard and house just in case."

"I'm glad," Alexa said. "Until they convict Blaine and put him in jail, I won't feel totally safe."

"I know," I said and squeezed her hand. "They will put him away. Maybe he'll accept a plea bargain and accept a lesser charge and will go to jail. Then, he'll be out of our hair for a while."

"I hope so," Alexa replied, her tone doubtful. "If he does go to jail, he'll be even more resentful of me and you." She shook her head. "Why couldn't he just get a life and leave me alone?"

"He's one of those guys who can't let go," I said, remembering what I'd read about stalkers. "He's obsessed. Don't worry — they'll put him away. I have faith in the justice system."

"For how long?"

"He raped and assaulted you and stalked you and posted that video, plus he assaulted Candace, so if they could nail him for that, it would be attempted murder. He'd go away for life."

"He has nothing to lose then, does he?" Alexa glanced at me, her eyes wide. "That makes him even more dangerous."

I leaned over and kissed her. "Like you said, we don't need to worry. We have the very best in personal security. You're safe. As safe as you can be."

She sighed, and I could tell she was spooked and wasn't really convinced by what she said but was putting on a brave face. "Maybe we should move to Brussels and get away from the US."

I frowned, for I really didn't think the move to Brussels was best for all of us. Before I could speak, she held up a hand.

"I'm kidding," she said. "I don't want to go to Brussels. It's just that I highly doubt Blaine would make the effort to follow me there."

"Look," I said and kissed her knuckles. "You're safe. As soon as the guard thought there was the slightest risk, you were brought inside, and the place was locked down."

"How is that any way to live?"

"Alexa," I said and shook my head, angry that Blaine was ruining things for Alexa. "The Prosecutor will send him to prison. Until then, you're safe. Today should prove that to you."

She forced a smile and nodded finally, but I knew she still didn't feel completely safe. I knew that there was really nothing more I could do to convince her, so instead, I intended to spend as much time with her and Leif as I could and keep the trips to the city at a minimum.

Luckily, we could always do FaceTime calls if anything important came up. Other than our trip to the city on Saturday for the meeting with Hanson and the other investors, we had nothing major on the agenda for Astra and anything that did come up could be handled via conference call or video.

Once the police had finished their work and had carted the two hoods off to the local police station, we spent the rest of the evening sitting on the patio, discussing the deal and how it would be structured so that we created a new entity that would invite even further investment from other players in the aerospace industry who wanted to get in on the future.

"It means I won't have to move to Houston and will only have to visit when there's an annual meeting or when we have a launch at the nearby facility. I'll stay in New York and run Astra, focusing on our part of the project."

"Communications tech, right?" Alexa asked. She knew as much as anyone what Astra's role would be. We had made our name in communications tech for the military, but now, that tech would be used in launches. There were other investors, like Hanson, who had expertise in rocketry who would focus on developing that technology. Each different partner in the consortium would provide their own expertise and we would all contribute to the project and benefit based on that contribution. No one single company could do it all. Mining the asteroid belt was a huge historic challenge that would push technology forward. It would take at least a decade to get there if we all worked together.

That was the hope and the plan.

When I leaned back with Alexa beside me later that night after Leif went to bed and we were sitting on the patio side by side, I felt like life was finally as close to perfect as it could be.

I took Alexa's hand and squeezed it, bringing her knuckles to my lips for a kiss.

"I'm blissfully happy," I said, and met her eyes.

"Me, too," she replied and for once that day, I saw that she was relaxed and really was happy.

That made it all worthwhile.

CHAPTER 22

Alexa

On Saturday, my parents arrived in the afternoon before Luke and I were scheduled to leave for the city and the party with Hanson and the other investors.

While Luke and I dressed, my mother and father took turns spoiling Leif. I stood in the walk-in closet and stared at my reflection in the full-length mirror. I wore my coral blue dress that had a bit more room in the hips to accommodate my post-baby spread.

"You look gorgeous," Luke said, coming up behind me, his arms around my waist. He caressed my body, his eyes on my reflection in the mirror. "Your breasts are magnificent. I wish we had more time before we left. I could take you right here and right now..."

I smiled and felt my cheeks heat at the sound of desire in his voice.

"We have the entire night alone at the apartment," I said, my voice a bit husky with desire for him.

"I can't wait," he said and kissed my neck.

He glanced at his watch when it chimed, indicating that the limo was in the driveway. He sighed. "Time to go, M'Lady. Our coach awaits."

I turned around and slipped my arms around his neck, pressing against his body. "I'm so glad everything worked out and we're celebrating the deal instead of mourning it like we thought we'd be doing this weekend."

"Me, too," Luke replied.

We left the bedroom and went downstairs where my parents were playing with Leif on the living room floor. I knew once we left, they'd take turns carrying him around the yard, and generally doing indulgent grandparent things.

Leif was in good hands and would be cared for royally.

I'd banked some pumped breastmilk servings the previous two days, so there were lots in the freezer. Hopefully, they wouldn't have any problems with Leif, and we would all enjoy our getaways — Luke and I with grownups in Manhattan and Mom and Dad enjoying some grandparent time with Leif at the beach house.

"Our limo has arrived," I said when I got to the living room. "We're off. Enjoy your time with Leif. Call us if you need to."

"We'll be fine, dear," my mother said, smiling up at me. "You two have the time of your life at your celebration. Don't even think of us. We raised you, after all. We know a thing or two about babies."

"I know," I said and bent down to stroke Leif's little still-very-bald baby head. "I'll call you later jut to check in."

"Okay, sweetheart," my father replied, smiling. "Go. Do some grownup things."

Luke said goodbye and we left the beach house and went down the steps to our waiting limo. The driver was standing at the door, waiting for us to get inside.

"Mr. and Mrs. Marshall," he said, his hand waving to the interior. "There's a bottle of champagne inside."

"Thanks," Luke said and helped me inside.

I crept into my seat and waited until Luke got in beside me. Once he was inside, we fastened our seatbelts and Luke removed the cork from the bottle of champagne.

"You agreed to have a couple of glasses," he said, reminding me that I had decided to have a drink or two to celebrate the deal. I'd have processed the alcohol by the time I had to nurse Leif, so I figured I could indulge for at least one night.

"I did," I said and smiled, accepting the glass of champagne from him.

"To the deal," Luke said and held up his glass of bubbly. "May it be the most successful joint venture in space ever and get us to the asteroid belt within the decade."

"To the deal," I replied and held up my own glass. We clinked glasses and then took a sip of the champagne. I made a face as the bubbles tickled my palate. "This is tasty. I never liked champagne when I was younger, but this I could drink."

"That's because you grew up drinking the bad kind," Luke said. "This is the good kind, and it is very tasty."

***

The drive into Manhattan went fast and before I knew it, we were at the venue — a high-end restaurant in the financial district which had a view of the Hudson River and a small park at the edge of the water.

"This is nice," I said as we stepped out of the limo and

stood looking out at the river. "Do I look expensive enough for this place?"

"You look perfect," Luke said and took my hand, pulling me closer for a kiss.

I exhaled and glanced down at my body, at the small swell around my middle from pregnancy that stubbornly wouldn't leave even though I was nursing. From what my midwife told me, nursing helped the body return to normal because of the drain on your bodily resources. Apparently, I was eating more than enough to maintain my weight.

We walked into the restaurant's cool interior, and I glanced around, feeling suddenly very conspicuous. Our table was in a separate part of the restaurant and had access to a patio. The weather was a bit cool at night, so the guests were inside but the patio doors were thrown open to admit the breeze and it was lovely.

Luke and Hanson shook hands and then we said hello to everyone before sitting down. John was there with Felicia, Frank Campbell had his wife, Adam Pierce even had his wife, Carol, present for the celebration. And of course, Elena. She was seated close to Jack, who was gazing at her adoringly.

"Hello, Luke, Alexa," Elena said, her voice high and loud. "Alexa, how lovely you look — and so soon after having a baby. Don't worry, my sister said that she got back to her pre-pregnancy weight at about a year postpartum." Elena smiled brightly, tilting her head to the side.

"I think Alexa looks positively glowing," Adam Pierce said and pulled out a chair for me.

"Thank you," I said and sat beside him. Luke said on the other side of me. Across from me, Elena drank her glass of champagne, eyeing me from over the top of her champagne glass.

What a bitch...

I would never ever mention a woman's post-baby weight. It was a direct dig at my figure, and I felt a tiny smidgen of pain creep in, underneath the disgust at her for being such a bitch.

"Don't worry, Elena," Luke said and put his arm over my shoulder. "One day, you might meet your own knight in shining armor and get married, have a family. I'm sure glad Alexa and I met. It's quite the story." Luke gazed down into my eyes, and we shared a secret smile.

"Do tell us," Jack said, leaning forward. "I love a good romantic meeting story. How did you two meet?"

I raised my eyebrows. Was Luke really going to tell the truth?

While I listened, he did recount most of the details of our meeting and how I pretended to be the escort he hired to shame his cheating brother-in-law.

"I don't take kindly to men who cheat, especially on their pregnant wives," Luke said and raised his glass of champagne. "Or the women who cheat with them."

"That's quite the story," Elena said. "Pretending to be an escort? Did he pay you, at least?"

"I did it out of the kindness of my heart," I said, shaking my head. "Dinner and drinks at the venue was fun and we all went out dancing together afterwards."

I turned to John and Felicia, who held up their glasses. "It was a night to remember," John said. "Luke was smitten that night and it was a no-brainer that they'd get together in the end."

"How sweet," Elena said and gave me a fake smile. The fakest smile I think I'd ever seen on a woman in response to a sweet romantic meeting. "It must have been hard for you to give up your studies for new motherhood. You never did finish your dissertation, right? So many young women give up careers for motherhood. I couldn't imagine it, frankly. I would never want to be dependent on a man for my subsistence."

I could practically see the hatred in her green eyes.

"Our story was really sweet," I replied. "We pretended to be a couple but couldn't keep up the charade, so we became one. The rest is, as they say, history. As to my dissertation, it's almost done, and I intend to finish it. Luke and I decided to each take a year leave of absence to be full-time parents. There will still be a Columbia when the year is up and of course, the consortium will just be getting going."

"What a great story you two have," Ken Hanson said, raising his glass. "Elena, why on earth aren't you married yet? A woman of your achievements? You were one of the only female entrepreneurs in the aerospace industry back in the day when you started. I expect most of the nerds were tripping over their tongues to impress you, if I remember my Silicon Valley tech bros correctly..."

"I haven't met that special someone yet, I suppose," Elena said with a light laugh, holding her glass up. "Maybe I'll get lucky and finally meet Mr. Right in the consortium."

"Here's to that," Ken said and toasted Elena. "There's still hope for you. You must be in your mid-thirties, right? That's not too late to become a mother, with today's technology. Even if you don't find Mr. Right."

Elena fake smiled so hard, I actually felt bad for her. For a brief *brief* moment. Then, I didn't.

She was the one who brought up the whole business of motherhood. I had a sneaking suspicion that while she craved limelight, and enjoyed when all the eyes were on her, she didn't like her age and status as a single woman to be the focus of everyone's attention.

The rest of the evening went smoothly, and Elena seemed a bit subdued, perhaps feeling the sting of being the only woman at the table without a date or a husband. I was surprised that she didn't bring along a boy toy to wear on her arm for show at least, but I guess it would be hard for a hired man to compete with the tech and aerospace giants sitting at the table.

I guessed Elena didn't feel any feminine solidarity with the other women at the table. She must have seen herself as separate from the rest of us who weren't directly involved in the venture but were there with our partners. Still, to be so openly catty...

I had thought a tech gal would be better than that, but I figured I was wrong. She was as catty as any non-tech woman I had ever met. She should feel better than me because she was one of the boys, but she clearly didn't.

I truly almost felt sorry for her.

Almost.

We spent an hour after dinner in the restaurant's bar, and there was an hour we actually spent playing pool on one of the three pool tables in the back. I excused myself and went to the washroom towards the end of the evening and was in a stall when I heard Elena and Carol, come into the washroom. I sat quietly as I heard them speaking.

Elena had to know I was in the washroom.

"Did you see the maternity dress she was wearing? How did he ever get trapped by a woman like her?"

Carol responded, her voice a conspiratorial whisper. "I think she's in here..."

There was a shocked gasp and then water ran, and I think I heard a giggle, which I assumed was Elena's, although given how she was making adoring eyes at Elena all night, it could also have been Carol.

I left the stall and came out, standing directly beside Elena.

"Oh, you're here," Elena said. "I was just saying how lovely your dress was." She smiled, like she didn't care that I knew she was lying.

I decided to say nothing because I knew my voice would have wavered with emotion. I simply washed my hands and left the washroom.

I felt humiliated, but at the same time, I knew that Elena disliked me for some reason and was being catty.

Why?

Did she have a crush on Luke or something?

I couldn't figure it out. I made my way back to the table where Luke was deep in a conversation with Adam. I glanced over and saw Elena and Carol at one of the pool tables, playing.

Good. I didn't want to have to face either of them, knowing what they said to me. Elena was a small petty female to comment on my dress that way.

Luke reached over and took my hand, squeezing it under the table, giving me a quick affectionate smile.

'You want to get out of here?' he mouthed when Adam was turned away, glancing at his wife by the pool table.

I nodded. *'Good'* he replied.

He stood up and fastened his jacket. "Well, Adam," Luke said. "It's been a real pleasure getting together with you and the gang tonight, but my beautiful wife and I are both exhausted after being new parents for the past week and need our beauty sleep."

Adam stood and he and Luke shook hands. "I totally understand," he said. "Thanks for coming and for the enjoyable evening with us. I look forward to meeting with you this week to work on the details of the deal."

"Me as well," Luke said.

"Give our regards to the pool players when they get back," I said when Adam shook my hand.

"I will," Adam said and winked at me. "Good night."

Then, we left.

"Thank God," Luke said and pulled me out of the restaurant to the street where the limo was waiting. "I was bored to tears with Adam telling me about his last trip to Montana to go fly fishing…"

"At least he has a passion," I said with a smile.

"Yes," Luke said when we finished fastening our seat-belts. "I have one, too. You."

He kissed me as the limo drove off.

I knew that whatever Elena or Carol — or anyone thought — that Luke found me desirable and loved me, maternity dress or not.

CHAPTER 23

Luke

THE NEXT DAY I SPENT A COUPLE OF HOURS IN THE office, while Alexa recuperated at the apartment.

While I was sitting at my desk, going over the financial sheets John had provided for my signature, I heard a knock at the door and Adam Pierce poked his head in.

"Do you mind?" he asked, pointing to the chair across from my desk. "There wasn't a receptionist outside, so I took the liberty..."

I stood and waved him in. "Of course, Adam," I said, and we went to the sofa against the wall by the windows. "You're always welcome. My receptionist is off today. I'm on my own."

He sat and adjusted his jacket. "Good time last night," he said and nodded. "I enjoyed our dinner and the chance to meet everyone involved."

"Me, too," I said. "It was a fun night."

S. E. LUND

He smiled and then he looked uncomfortable, like he had something difficult to say.

"Is there a problem, Adam?"

"Well, yes, there is. I don't really know how to say this, but Carol told me after we left the venue that Elena had been saying really nasty things about Alexa to her all night and once, when they were in the washroom, Elena said something nasty while Alexa was in the washroom. Carol was really offended, but tried not to look it because of course, Elena is one of our partners. I wanted you to know that I'm considering kicking her off the board and out of the deal. I needed you to know just in case it was a problem."

A shock went through me. "Alexa never said anything, but I guess she didn't want to do anything that might cause problems, but that's clearly unacceptable."

Adam nodded. "Carol couldn't let it go and I agree. I wouldn't accept a male colleague making comments about one of the partner's wives. I don't think it's right for Elena to do so."

"I'm fine if you want to remove her from the board. How much of a hit will we take if she pulls out of the deal?"

Adam shook his head. "Not much," he replied. "If we have Hanson on, we don't need Elena and her harassment."

"Good," I said and shook my head. "I can't believe Alexa didn't say anything. I'm sure she was hurt because she's sensitive about her post-baby weight."

"Alexa is a very intelligent and capable young woman, and you should be proud," Adam said. "Anyway, that's all I really wanted to say other than I'm glad we had the dinner together."

He stood and we shook hands and I escorted him out of the office to the elevator. We spoke about our next meeting and then I said goodbye as he took the elevator down.

～

WHEN I ARRIVED BACK at the hotel, Alexa had packed up our bags and was waiting to go back to the beach house.

"How was your morning?" she asked and slipped her arms around me.

"Very interesting," I said and led her to the bed. I sat her down and sat beside her, taking her hand. "I had a surprise meeting with Adam Pierce this morning. He wanted to let me know he was going to kick Elena off the board and out of the deal."

Alexa frowned. "Why? What happened? I thought she was one of Seneca's partners and is on their board."

"She was, but Carol came to Adam after the dinner and said Elena was talking about you in a very nasty way, and even while you were in the washroom. Why didn't you say anything to me?"

Alexa closed her eyes. "Because what she said was true. I'm not from your world. I'm not from wealth. I still have excess baby weight that I can't seem to shake." Tears escaped her eyes.

I took her chin in my hand and turned her to face me. "You are the most beautiful, wonderful woman I've ever known. I love you. You should have told me. It was unacceptable for Elena to be so nasty and shows that she lacks the kind of professionalism we need on the board and as part of the deal. She's gone as of today."

Alexa smiled through her tears. "I felt so embarrassed that she had such a low opinion of me, and I wanted to tell you, but I didn't want it to become a problem for the deal."

I pulled her into my arms and kissed her warmly. "Never hold anything back, okay? We have to be completely open with each other so there's no distance between us."

"Okay," she said, her face serious. "Could you remember to hit the laundry basket when you take off your boxer briefs at night, so I don't have to pick them up? I mean, if we're being totally open with each other..." Then, her eyes narrowed, and I knew she was joking.

I laughed out loud. "I asked for it," I said and kissed her.

A COUPLE of weeks flew by as Alexa and I spent most of our time with Leif, walking the beach and caring for him as he grew and met one milestone after another.

The deal with Hanson was progressing, and although it was still in the planning stages, I felt as though it was fast becoming a reality. Hanson knew a lot of high rollers who wanted in on the future, and so we signed on more partners in the joint venture. Each partner had a specific expertise in the area or just saw the venture as a solid investment.

Whatever the case, I met with Ken frequently on Zoom and went over the developments and plans for the first steps the consortium would take to make the dream real.

"One of our new investors suggested something the other day that I want you to consider. He thinks that the first thing we should do is test out mining on the moon," Ken said to me one day when we were both sitting in front of our computers on a conference call. "What do you think of a moon base that was designed to mine there first? It's a helluva lot closer and there are valuable metals on the moon that could easily be transported back to Earth."

"The moon?" I said, frowning. "I've known that it had

valuable metals, but my sights were always on the asteroid belt. But I'm intrigued. Tell me more."

We spent an hour just talking through the idea, and in the end, I felt it was a good one. It would be proof of concept. We could develop the mining equipment on the moon and then see how it performed in low-G for when it went to the asteroid belt itself.

In the end, I was sold on the idea and was glad that things had worked out between Hanson and Astra. It almost hadn't.

When the conference call was finished, I went into the kitchen where Alexa was fixing lunch and came up behind her, slipping my arms around her waist. Behind us, Leif was sitting at the island in his chair, playing with toys.

"How's it going?" Alexa asked, turning her head for a quick kiss. "Did you and Ken have a good discussion?"

"We did, and guess what? We're going to the Moon..."

"What?"

Alexa turned around in my arms and her eyes were wide. "The Moon? What about the asteroid belt?"

"That, too, but first, the Moon. We'll develop the tech there to ensure it functions well in low-G. Then, it's the belt."

She narrowed her eyes. "I don't suppose you're planning on taking a trip there or anything..."

I smiled, because of course I had thought that very thing. "Not until Leif is older and doesn't care about me anymore, just in case there is an unfortunate accident..."

"What about me?" she asked, pouting. "When I first met you, you were ready to go to Mars and leave Earth behind. Then, I thought you were happy to stay on Earth because of us."

"I was. I am. But you have to realize, in the next decade,

going to the moon will be no more difficult or dangerous than a trip to the Himalayas or to the Rain Forest in Brazil. It's going to be common."

She sighed and adjusted my collar. "Just wait until it's really safe and you're certain to come back, okay? I don't want Leif to grow up without a father, even if he was a space pioneer and lost his life heroically while setting up a moon base."

"Don't worry," I said and pulled her closer, kissing her. "I'll wait until he is consumed with other things, like girls and whatever music is popular and whatever video game is the best seller before I go. I want to come back, too, you know…"

She smiled. "Do you have to go into the city today? I was hoping we could take a nice walk along the beach and have a barbecue."

"Today and then no meetings for an entire week. We can go for a sail tomorrow when your parents come to stay for the weekend. How does that sound?"

She nodded. "Okay. That sounds nice."

I was taking a trip into the city to meet with John and Adam Pierce. Hanson was in Houston and had meetings in the afternoon so that was why we met over Zoom in the morning. I called the limo service and then got my papers together and went to the door to pull on my shoes. Alexa brought Leif over to the front entrance for a kiss goodbye.

"There goes Mr. Big Daddy, to the city for his very important meetings," Alexa said.

"Mr. Big Daddy will be back for supper." I leaned down and kissed Leif on the head. Then, I kissed Alexa. "I'll call when I leave the city, so you know I'm on my way."

"Okay," she said and leaned up to kiss me one more time.

Then, I left, waving goodbye to the two of them before I sat in the back of the limo.

IT WAS when we were almost at the end of our road leading to the main highway back to the city that I saw a vehicle turning down our street. For some reason, I had a bad feeling about it, and I pressed the speaker button so I could speak to Stuart, the current driver from the security company.

"Hey, Stuart, can you turn around and follow that dark truck that just turned down the lane?"

"You mean the Ford?" Stuart asked.

"Yes, that's the one."

"Is there a problem?" he asked, pulling into an empty driveway and turning the limo around.

"I just have this feeling..."

"Roger that," Stuart said and drove back down the road leading to our property. Sure enough, the black pickup had stopped next to a small, wooded area a few houses down from our beach house and the driver was walking down a path to the beach. Maybe he was just visiting so he could walk the beach, but why would he park his truck there and walk to the beach when there was a public parking lot a mile further down the coast?

"Can you call in the plates?"

"I can," Stuart replied and spoke into his cell. I opened my door to get out of the limo and Stuart stopped me. "Sir, I'd advise you to remain in the vehicle. I'll investigate, if needed."

"I want to see where he's going," I said, ignoring his

advice. I followed him down the path and saw that he was walking down the beach towards the beach house.

It might be completely innocent. Maybe he lived in the area and was just taking a walk, but why the dark hoodie covering his head and the dark sunglasses? It was a cloudy day...

"Sir, can I ask you to stay back? I called the plates in and it's a stolen vehicle reported this morning from Queens. I've already called the guard at the beach house and they're on lockdown."

"Great," I said and took out my cell.

Then, I thought better of it, and stood back, watching as Stuart chased down the man and confronted him. They got into a pushing and shoving match, and before I knew it, Stuart had the man on the ground, his face in the sand, his arms in cuffs behind his back.

It was useful to have a former cop as a driver...

I ran up to the two of them and watched as Stuart reached into the man's pants pocket and pulled out a wallet.

"Says his name is Garrett L. Bowen of Queens."

"Turn him over," I said and watched as Stuart did, flipping the guy over onto his back so we could see the man's face.

He had longish hair, a scruffy beard and moustache.

Garrett L. Bowen of Queens, apparently.

Who the hell was he and why was he out here with a stolen vehicle? And why did this keep happening?

It seemed too much of a coincidence that he was close to our beach house, but then again, he could have been just scouting out rich homes to break into and steal from. Our place might not have been the target.

I hoped that was it.

I was getting a bit too paranoid about Blaine still being

out there. His trial couldn't come fast enough, and I cursed the slowness of the justice system, even as I was glad that we had one of the best in the world.

The police showed up within ten minutes, and took over from Stuart, who had to give police a statement, and then I had to give one as well. I sat in the police cruiser and told them what happened from my perspective, and then asked the one cop to call me when they had any information.

I told him about the situation with Blaine and that if there was any connection between the two men, I would like to know.

"Is there a reason you think they may be connected?" the cop asked.

"No," I said and shook my head. "But I know he's out to get my wife and hurt her and her family members, so I wouldn't put it past him to hire someone to hurt us."

The cop almost smiled but held it back. "That's possible, of course, but we have an ongoing problem with break-ins in the wealthier neighborhoods."

"Of course, you're right," I said and shook my head. I realized I was being paranoid. This was probably a small-time hood from Queens who was out looking for computers, flat screens and other valuables to pawn for money for his drugs.

At least, I hoped that was the case...

I went back to the limo and called Alexa, letting her know what had happened.

"Do you want me to cancel the meeting and come stay with you?" I asked, hearing the sound of nerves in her voice.

"No, no," she said quickly. "You go ahead. I'm safe here with the guard on duty. We'll have a nice supper on the patio when you get back. How about grilled Greek chicken and vegetables?"

"Sounds great," I said. "If you're sure."

"I'm sure."

I ended the call and told Stuart to continue into the city, glad that we'd stopped and checked on the suspicious man and vehicle. While Alexa would have been safe regardless, it was good to stop a potential robber before he had the chance to strike.

WE ARRIVED IN THE CITY, and I spent the afternoon meeting with John and Adam Pierce to go over the latest news on the investors who had joined once Ken Hanson made it known that he had partnered with Astra to create the consortium. Apparently, he had a lot of people interested in getting a piece of the future with us and before we knew it, the consortium had grown and doubled the initial investment dollars.

The deal was perhaps the biggest in the history of the aerospace industry outside the initial investments in the Apollo mission.

It was an exciting time to be involved in the industry and I felt it would be my legacy. From the time I was just a boy and my father and mother had given me my first telescope, I had my eyes on the stars and had wanted to go out into space.

I wouldn't be going there any time soon — I had Alexa and Leif here on Earth to keep my feet on solid ground — but one day, maybe I would. Until then, I could be part of building the industry that would eventually go to space and make it part of humanity's future.

CHAPTER 24

Alexa

NOT LONG AFTER LUKE SAID GOODBYE, THE GUARD from the guardhouse called me and when I saw his name and number on my call display, I felt a shock of adrenaline go through me.

"Yes?"

"Ma'am, we have a possible intruder on the property. Please take Leif to the safe room and wait for my all-clear."

"Right away," I said and grabbed Leif and went right into the room we designated the "safe room," which was next to the stairs beside the furnace room. I closed the door and sat with Leif on my lap, waiting.

I had a stash of toys in there and a lamp, plus I had my cell. While I waited, Leif played with one of the toys he hadn't seen for quite a while and was happy, stuffing it into his mouth in as many ways as he could.

I grabbed my cell and called Luke right away. He answered, and his voice was breathless.

"Luke," I said. "They just called us and we're in lockdown. Leif and I are in the safe room."

"Good," he said. "I'm going to find out who this sonofabitch is and punch his lights out."

"Luke!" I said, alarmed. "Don't you dare! What if he has a gun? Don't worry about me. The house is in lockdown, and Leif and I are in the safe room. Leave the policing to the police, okay?"

"All right. I'll call you back when I know more. Sit tight. You're safe."

"Okay. Be careful."

"I will."

With that, Luke ended the call. I had a struggle to hold Leif and type at the same time, but managed to send Luke a text, my hand shaking just a bit from anxiety. I knew I was safe with three guards monitoring the property, but still, I didn't want Luke to take matters into his own hands. It unnerved me that there would be anyone trying to break into the property. There were clear no-trespassing signs on the walls bordering the property, there were security cameras, and there was a guard gate with passcode required to enter.

Who would be fool enough to think they could enter the property and get away with it?

About ten minutes later, I got another call from Luke. He told me about the identity of the prowler — some young guy from Queens.

"Do you want me to cancel the meeting and come stay with you?" he asked, probably hearing the sound of nerves in my voice.

"No, no," I said quickly. "You go ahead. I'm safe here

with the guard on duty. We'll have a nice supper on the patio when you get back. How about grilled Greek chicken and vegetables?"

"Sounds great," he said. "If you're sure."

"I'm sure."

I heard a knock at the door to the safe room. "Yes?"

"It's me, Ma'am," the guard said. "We got the all-clear. You can come out now."

"Thank you," I said and let out a huge sigh of relief. I unlocked the door and left the alcove, emerging from the small room into the main hallway. I glanced out the windows beside the front entrance and saw a police car with lights flashing on the road outside the property. There were several other vehicles as well.

"What's happening now?"

"Local police are taking reports from the guards on duty, and they'll do a canvass of the neighborhood for any video of the vehicle and suspect. They'll take the suspect into the local precinct, and process him, charge him with trespassing and whatever else they can get him on."

"Anything on my end?" I asked, wondering if I'd have to speak to someone.

"No, Ma'am," he said. "They're dealing with us as Mr. Marshall requested. He didn't want you to be questioned, and since you didn't even see the suspect, they don't need your report. We'll take care of it."

"Great," I said, relieved that I wouldn't have to speak with police. Besides, I didn't see anything and all I did was go into the safe room and wait.

WHEN THE EXCITEMENT and fear had died down from the morning's events, I spent time on the patio reading the latest article in the international relations policy journal I subscribed to. Although I wasn't working on my dissertation, I still was interested in keeping up with developments and so I received a monthly journal and read it with interest.

Around two in the afternoon, while Leif was down for his nap and Luke was in the city at his meeting, I received an email from Professor Turner, and read it with interest.

Dear Alexa:

Just to let you know that I sent your CV to a friend of mine who works at the UN as part of the UN's Office for the Coordination of Humanitarian Affairs (OCHA). He's the Assistant Director and is looking for a temp part-time Policy Advisor in October when his current Advisor comes back from Maternity Leave and wants to job share. I think the job is right up your alley and told him about you and your work in the area. He seemed really interested. You could work part-time for the OCHA and get some great experience under your belt. I sang your praises and so don't be surprised if his office doesn't contact you and offer you the temp position starting in November. I know that's still a bit sooner than you planned on going back to work, but it would be only two and a half days a week for a year.

Take care and let me know if he contacts you and what you decide.

Cheers,

Helen

I read the letter over again and again, and then did some Googling of the Office for the Coordination of Humanitarian Affairs and the current Assistant Director, who was Helen's friend. The job sounded amazing and would deal with issues of displacement during conflict and disasters, preparing policy position papers and monitoring countries and areas that had potential for humanitarian crises leading to displacement.

In other words, it was right up my alley.

I felt a surge of excitement and wrote her back right away.

Dear Helen,

Thanks so much for forwarding my CV to your friend in the OCHA. The job sounds fantastic and with it being part-time, it would be a great way to get experience and ease back into the working world after my maternity leave. I could work on my dissertation and work part-time, so if your friend is truly interested in me, then by all means, tell him I would be very excited at the opportunity.

Thanks again for thinking of me and for the job offer.

Sincerely,

Alexa

I sent the email off and then got up and started fixing things for supper, marinating the chicken breasts, and cutting up the potatoes and marinating them in the same Greek marinade I made from a recipe I got off my favorite Instagram recipe page. I made a salad and then heard snuffling sounds from Leif over the baby monitor, and so I went to get him up from his nap.

His cheeks were rosy and there was a big smile on his face when he saw me.

"There you are, my little man," I said and picked him up. He was soaking wet and so I changed him and brought him out to the patio, where I fed him and then put him in his activity chair so he could play with his toys while I read over material about the OCHA. Luke was scheduled to be home in about fifteen minutes and then we'd have a drink before supper and Luke would grill the chicken, vegetables and potatoes.

I was excited to be able to tell him about the potential job with the UN in Manhattan. I checked my cell and decided to text Luke, so I knew when he was on his way.

ALEXA: Hey, any update?

LUKE: Yes, I spoke to the police officer who has the case. They figure the suspect — some guy named Bowen — stupidly thought the property was empty and he could come in and steal some expensive electronics before the security company arrived.

ALEXA: I'm sure he's just some local hood or something, hoping for a computer or flatscreen they could pawn for drug money. It's just this is happening too often. I thought we'd be safer out here than in the city, but now I'm thinking your penthouse apartment in Manhattan is safer than we are out here.

LUKE: I'd hate to leave the beach house. It's so great to be close to the ocean, so Leif can grow up on the beach... But if you really feel that way, we could move into the city. The penthouse is big enough if we want to live there. I'm not sure about schools in the neighborhood though. That could be a problem.

ALEXA: We could find somewhere else in a good neighborhood. What about Brooklyn?

LUKE: Brooklyn would be nice. We have time to decide. I'm leaving in half an hour, so should be there by six or six thirty.

ALEXA: I'll let you finish up. Text me just as you leave the building, okay?

LUKE: Okay. XO

ALEXA: OX

I sighed and stood at the patio doors, looking out at the

yard. Despite the wall that surrounded the property and the security cameras and alarm system and guards, I didn't really feel safe.

I GOT a text from Luke around four in the afternoon letting me know he was just getting into the vehicle. I had the chicken skewers marinating in the Greek dressing, as well as the vegetables, and there was a fresh loaf of bread waiting in tinfoil to be warmed up on the side of the grill. Luke would want a beer and to rest for half an hour before he started to grill so I planned that we would eat by seven thirty.

Leif was playing in his activity chair when I heard the ding of an arrival at the gate and knew Luke was back. It had taken him a little bit longer to get out of the city, so the traffic must have been heavy.

He came in the front entrance, and so I went to meet him.

"There you are," I said and watched as he removed his shoes and jacket. He came right over to me, and we embraced and kissed. "I'm so glad to see you."

"I'm so glad to be home. I'm sorry about the whole business this morning and that you had to spend the day alone."

"Don't even mention it. We had a very good day, other than the prowler. Come in. I have a nice cold beer waiting for you."

Luke followed me inside and went right over to pick up Leif and give him a kiss and hug.

"How's my little man?" Luke said and kissed Leif several times. "How did he do being stuck in the safe room?"

"He was fine. Totally oblivious. As long as he has toys, he's a happy camper."

"Good," Luke said. He sat at the kitchen island while I got him a beer from the refrigerator. "I've been thinking all day. Maybe it would be better to move into the city during the year and only come out here when the weather's good."

"Are you sure?" I said, feeling bad that we would be leaving, although it honestly made me feel safer thinking of living in the penthouse.

"I am," Luke said. "That way, I'd only be fifteen minutes away from the office so I could nip in to sign something or have a meeting without disrupting the whole day."

"I'm game," I said, glad that we would be moving back to the city.

We took our drinks and went out to the patio. Luke put Leif in his activity chair and then Luke and I sat in the two recliners and watched the ocean. I told Luke about the email I got from Professor Turner.

"That's great," Luke said. "I hope they call you for an interview." He held up his bottle of beer. I tapped my bottle of non-alcoholic wine spritzer against his in a toast. "To you getting a great part-time job at the UN."

"Cheers," I said and smiled, feeling excitement at the prospect that I might get an interview.

As we watched the sun set over the ocean, I felt certain that moving into the city would make it easier on us all.

After Luke had time to decompress, I gave Leif his final feed of the evening. We both gave him a bath and then put him to bed for the night. Luke grilled the chicken and vegetables while I got the rest of the meal ready.

We sat at the table and served ourselves, the scent of the food making me salivate.

"It smells so good," Luke said and dished out some of the Greek salad to us both.

Just then, Luke's cell rang. When he checked the call display, it was from the local police department. He put it on speakerphone so we could both hear.

"Hello," Luke said.

"Hello, Mr. Marshall? This is Sergeant Bruce Townsend of the Westhampton Beach Police Department. I'm handling the prowler case regarding your property."

"Yes, this is Luke Marshall. What news have you got for me? What can you tell me about this Bowen fellow who tried to break into my property?"

"I just wanted you to know that we've connected Mr. Bowen to a person of interest to you and your wife, Alexa Dixon Marshall. We were able to examine Bowen's cellphone and found several dozen contacts with Blaine Northrup of Portland, Oregon, over the preceding three weeks, who is currently out on bail. I thought you would like to know. I can't give you any more details because of the ongoing case, but just wanted you to be aware."

My eyes widened at that. That bastard...

"Thank you," Luke said and frowned, glancing at me. "That's good to know. We've been extra careful about security because of Mr. Northrup. Do you think they'll be able to charge Mr. Northrup with conspiracy to commit a crime or anything? I mean, it's no coincidence that the prowler was trying to get into our property and knows Northrup."

"No, it's not just a coincidence. I'm sure that police will be trying to elicit as much information from Bowen about the plan to break into the property and will know more in the coming days. Just thought you would like to know that there's a connection."

"Yes, very interested in that. Thanks for calling. Please call if you can update me on any further developments."

"I will," Townsend said and ended the call.

Luke turned to me. "Damn Blaine. He's been in contact with Bowen and there were dozens of calls between them over the past few weeks."

"My God, when will that man ever give up?" I said, anger at Blaine filling me. "If Bowen knows Blaine, there's no way he wasn't in this with Blaine, trying to scare me."

"Or Blaine knows there might be some good electronics at our place and simply figured it was a good place to break into."

"You're being too charitable. If Blaine was willing to push Candace onto the tracks, I suspect he was willing to pay this Bowen guy money to attack me — maybe even kill me."

Luke reached across the table and took my hand in his. "We're safe now," he said. "Police know about it and Bowen will probably confess and implicate Blaine if it helps reduce his own sentence. There is no honor among thieves, and so if Blaine was behind this, we'll probably know soon enough. Let's forget about Blaine and the whole business and focus on the great news from Professor Turner and the prospect of a job at the UN. And moving into the city."

Across from him, I sighed heavily and finally nodded. "Yes. I won't let that bastard ruin my life."

We held up our bottles once more and toasted each other.

After we cleaned up from dinner, we spent the rest of the evening on the patio with the sound system playing some old gold we both enjoyed and tried to appreciate the warm evening and clear sky over the ocean. It would be hard to forget about Blaine and what happened. Blaine would remain a threat for as long as he was free. I hoped the hood implicated Blaine because he would be taken right into custody and kept there until his trial for breaching the terms of his bail.

When I checked my watch, it was already nine thirty. I couldn't help but yawn.

"You too tired to dance a bit?" Luke asked, standing and holding out his hand.

"Never too tired to dance with you," I replied and stood up, smiling and taking his hand. He pulled me into his arms, and we slow-danced to Yellow by Coldplay.

We spent the entire song in each other's embrace and the feel of his body pressed against mine, my head on his shoulder, aroused me. Luke pulled me more tightly against him and I glanced up, smiling. He was as aroused as I was.

Then, I took his hand and led him inside. Luke closed the sliding doors and locked them, then we went hand in hand up the stairs to the bedroom.

It was the perfect way to end what started off as a very bad day...

CHAPTER 25

Luke

Our move into the city took place over an entire week, and while I felt sad that we felt unsafe in the beach house, it was for the best. The penthouse was pretty sweet, all things considered. We had an amazing view of the city, and enough room for the three of us. Plus, when Alexa's parents came to babysit Leif while Alexa and I went sailing, they had their own bedroom.

Besides, it made my commute shorter and so we spent a couple of weeks acclimating to being back in the city.

We'd been in the penthouse for a couple of weeks when I got a call from Brian George.

"Hey," he said, his voice sounding gruff like a good PI should sound. "Just wanted you to know that the police are re-opening the case of the accident that killed your parents, based on the testimony of the guy who gave the jailhouse confession. They don't think your stepparents were involved, except that there was a disagreement about whether to work with the mobbed-up business. Apparently, your father said no. The Marshalls said yes. So, your parents were taken out to ensure the deal went through. I'm not sure if they can prove that your stepparents were implicated, but they're going to investigate. They'll do what they can, given the case is two decades old."

"Thanks for letting me know. Keep me informed, one way or the other."

"Will do," George said and ended the call.

I sighed and leaned back in my chair, wondering if my stepparents knew. I couldn't believe that they would have anything to do with killing my parents. Maybe the Russians made the decision on their own and took out my parents to ensure there was no way my father could scupper the deal.

Alexa came into the office and put her arms around my neck, kissing my cheek.

"What's up, Mr. Big Deal? You look so preoccupied."

I told her about the call I had with George.

She came around and sat on my lap, her arms around my shoulders. "That's terrible. Do you think they were involved?"

"I don't know, but if they were, I hope the police find out. But let's forget it. There's nothing I can do about it now, so I want to just put it out of my mind."

"Fine by me," she said and stroked my hair. "In the meantime, I have a little boy who wants a walk. Shall we go to the boardwalk and get in some afternoon sun before his nap?"

"Lead on, MacDuff," I said and followed her to the

living room, where Leif was busy playing in his activity chair.

***

Later, while Leif was sleeping and we were lazing around on the sofa, Alexa got a call from the contact at the UN about the part-time job. Of course, Alexa was only too happy to accept the offer of an interview, which was scheduled for one thirty in the afternoon on a bright Thursday in late September.

"I got it," Alexa said, her smile huge.

"Yay!" I replied and picked her up, twirling her around in a circle. "I knew they'd interview you for the job. They'd be crazy not to offer it to you on the spot."

We kissed and just when we were both passionately running our hands all over each other, a squeak came over the baby monitor.

We stopped what we were doing and looked into each other's eyes.

Then we both broke out laughing.

"Duty calls," Alexa said. "But you're mine tonight."

"I'm yours, tonight and always."

THAT THURSDAY, Alexa stood in front of the full-length mirror in the walk-in closet and turned from side to side. She was wearing a brand-new women's power suit she'd bought on a shopping trip with Candace earlier in the week during a girl's outing which included a spa appointment, shopping at a boutique and lunch. Her suit was nice. Black, with a bright white blouse underneath.

"Do I look like a Policy Advisor?" she asked, glancing at me and adjusting her jacket. I sat on the end of the bed in our bedroom, which had a view into the walk-in closet. Leif was sitting on my lap, playing with a toy.

"You look like a *Senior* Policy Advisor," I replied with a grin. "Don't think small."

She laughed. "It's only a plain Policy Advisor position and the pay is pretty low, but it's a start."

"The pay is fine," I replied, remembering the pay scale for that position that I'd read. Professor Turner had sent Alexa a job description which had the pay scale attached. It was pretty decent, all things considered. You needed a master's degree to even be interviewed, so that meant the pay scale was higher than the usual entry level policy job, but I told her she didn't have to worry about money.

"It's the principle of the thing," Alexa replied. "I don't want to be taken advantage of because I'm not finished my PhD. When I am, I can apply for Senior Policy Advisor positions."

I smiled and admired her ambition. She wasn't doing it for the money, but for the love, and I admired that. It was what guided me in my endeavors, and it was nice to have a partner who felt the same way about work and life in general.

I kissed her goodbye and waved Leif's hand as Alexa took the elevator down to the lobby where the limo was waiting to take her to the UN.

I could imagine how excited she must be at the prospect of interviewing for such a good job — probably as excited as I had been when signing the final papers that sealed the deal with Hanson and Seneca to create the business consortium for our joint venture.

For the next hour and a half, while I waited for Alexa to return, Leif and I went for a walk along the Hudson, enjoying the afternoon sun. If Alexa got the job, it would start in a mere four weeks, so I wanted to make sure we all had lots of together time before then. We were planning on going to the beach house on the weekend to go sailing, and the Dixons were arriving on Friday after lunch to sit with Leif. It would be one of our last weekends at the beach house and we were all excited about the trip.

We were no longer worried about staying at the beach house. Police had been able to elicit a confession from the hood that he and Blaine had conspired to break into the beach house, where the hood was planning doing more than just steal electronics or jewelry.

Blaine had hired him to kill Alexa.

The hood had accepted the money, and claimed he had no intention of killing her, but wanted to check the house out and see why Blaine was so crazy. We had no idea if his story was true, but whatever the case, it meant that Blaine was taken back into custody and would now be charged with conspiracy to commit first degree murder.

He would not be getting out anytime soon and that meant that finally, Alexa could relax.

LEIF and I arrived back at the penthouse, and I gave him a bottle of expressed breastmilk and then put him down for his afternoon nap. I spent some time cleaning up the kitchen, and then settled down in front of my laptop on the sofa, waiting for news from Alexa about how the job interview went.

Sure enough, around three thirty, I heard my cell ding and read the text from her.

ALEXA: *It went really well. They said they'd let me know on Monday.*

LUKE: Great! We can enjoy the weekend sailing and then you'll know one way or the other when we get back.

ALEXA: I hope I get it. It sounds really interesting. Perfect, in fact.

LUKE: I'm sure you're a great candidate. See you when you get home.

ALEXA: I'll be there in fifteen. Just got into the limo.

LUKE: Shall I order in?

ALEXA: You know it. Your choice. XO

LUKE: OX

I smiled as I imagined her ride back in the limo. She'd be feeling on top of the world, and so I decided to top it off with an order of Chinese from our favorite local restaurant.

When Alexa arrived, Leif was just waking up from his nap and so she went in and got him up, still wearing her power suit.

"There you are, my little man," she said and kissed him as she laid him on the change table. "Did you have fun with Mr. Big Daddy while I was out?"

"We had a nice time walking along the boardwalk."

"Good," Alexa said and when she was finished changing him, we all went into the kitchen where I poured us each something to drink — me some good craft beer, and Alexa her usual non-alcoholic wine spritzer.

"I think the interview went really well," Alexa said and held up her bottle. "They were really happy with the nature of my dissertation research and felt that we were a good match in terms of interests and research background."

"Good," I said and smiled. "Of course, they were impressed. You got scholarships and great grades. They'd be lucky to have you."

"I hope so."

For the rest of the night, we played with Leif and when

he went to bed, we played with each other until the two of us were both exhausted and fell asleep in each other's arms.

ON FRIDAY, we packed up our overnight bags and drove out to the beach house for the first time since we'd left, weeks earlier. We got settled in, and the Dixons arrived about an hour later. They were eager to have Leif to themselves while we went sailing on Saturday afternoon. We'd all spend the evening at the beach house, go sailing again on Sunday, and then return to the city on Sunday night.

While we were getting supper ready, Alexa got a call and took it, standing in the pantry, looking for something for the marinade. I went closer to the pantry door to listen and see who it was, and she turned and held her finger to her lip. She smiled, her eyes widening.

"Yes, of course, I would be exceptionally happy to accept the position. Yes, the first week in November would be perfect. I'll see you then. Thanks for calling."

I knew what that meant — they'd called and offered her the job early. They must have really liked her and decided not to wait on it.

"You got the job," I said and held out my arms.

"I did," she said and jumped into them, her arms around my neck. "They didn't want to wait for Monday, so they called right away after their interview of a candidate today, but they liked me best."

"That's amazing," I said and kissed her warmly. She kissed me back and then pulled away. "The first week in November. It's not too soon, is it? You'll be fine looking after Leif two and a half days a week without me?"

"Of course, I will. I'll be happy to. Besides, I know your

mom and dad will be happy to come over any time in case I need to go into the office."

She nodded. "Only too happy."

"Good," I said and stroked her cheek. "Let's go tell them the good news."

"Let's," she said and kissed me again. She grabbed a can of something off the shelf and left the pantry, pulling me behind her.

I followed her out onto the patio, and she could barely wait to tell them.

I stood and watched her hugging them both one after the other and knew that whatever trials we had been through with Blaine and Eric, our lives together were going to be amazing.

Once again, I thought about how lucky I was that I slipped up on the spelling of the email to Lexxi911.

That fateful typo and meeting Lexi911 instead had changed my life for the better.

I intended to make her life just as happy as mine had been for the rest of our lives.

THE END

ABOUT THE AUTHOR

S. E. Lund writes new adult, contemporary, erotic and paranormal romance. She lives on the side of Burke Mountain in beautiful British Columbia, Canada, with her family of animals and humans. She dreams of living in a place where snow is just a word in a dictionary.

You can find her website at:

www.selundauthor.com

She also writes crime thrillers as Susan Lund, featuring a romantic crime-fighting duo couple, crime reporter Tess McClintock and former FBI Special Agent Michael Carter:

www.susanlundbooks.com

For more information:

selund2012@gmail.com

ALSO BY S. E. LUND

New Adult Romance

THE BOYFRIEND SERIES DUOLOGY

Boy Toy: Book 1

Man Bun: Book 2

∼

THE MR BIG SERIES

Mr. Big Shot: Book 1

Mr. Big Love: Book 2

Mr. Big Daddy: Book 3

Mr. Big Deal: Book 4

∼

THE MACINTYRE BROTHERS SERIES

Tempt Me: Book 1

Tease Me: Book 2

Tame Me: Book 3

Tempting: The Collection

Contemporary Erotic Romance

THE UNRESTRAINED SERIES

The Agreement: Book 1

The Commitment: Book 2

Unrestrained: Book 3

Unbreakable: Book 4

Forever After: Book 5

Everlasting: Book 6

Drake Forever: Book 7

Endless: Book 8

The Unrestrained Series Collection 1 & 2

THE DRAKE SERIES (The Unrestrained Series from Drake's Point of View)

Drake Restrained

Drake Unwound

Drake Unbound

The Drake Series Collection

Military Romance / Romantic Suspense

THE BAD BOY SERIES

Bad Boy Saint: Book 1

Bad Boy Sinner: Book 2

Bad Boy Soldier: Book 3

Bad Boy Savior: Book 4

The Bad Boy Series Collection

Standalone Romances:

Matched: Standalone Romantic Comedy

If You Fall: Military Romance

Paranormal Romance

THE DOMINION SERIES

Dominion: Book 1 in the Dominion Series

Ascension: Book 2 in the Dominion Series

Retribution: Book 3 in the Dominion Series

Resurrection: Book 4 in the Dominion Series

Redemption: Book 5 in the Dominion Series

The Dominion Series Complete Collection: Books 1 - 5

THE ETERNITY SERIES

Eternity: Book 1